A Wishful Hope
An Aladdin Retelling
Sarah Beran

Contents

*For all those brave enough to shine light and hope into the
darkest places,
and for those who are seeking even just a glimmer of both.*

One

Dan

"Stop! Thief! Someone stop him!"

The cry carried above the din of the bustling market-place. Dan shielded his eyes against the hot desert sun as he craned his neck, attempting to search through the mass of brightly-colored canopies and milling people. Merchants behind their stands hawked their wares at passing buy-ers, who occasionally stopped to haggle over prices. Loud, boisterous peals of laughter came from the tables outside the tea shop on the corner, where Dan's new employer sat and enjoyed a steaming cup of chai.

Dan dropped his hand and shifted his hold on the crate of pomegranates, turning his attention back to stocking the fruit stand. He could feel Nasir's eyes on him, and he knew that the fruit seller, though he seemed to be distract-ed with his tea and his friends, was keeping a close, critical eye on his newest hire. Nasir was known for being hard to please. He had dismissed more than a few of Dan's friends with nothing more than a whipping and a scolding as their wages, but Dan was determined to do everything he could to keep his position.

Jasper's growing out of clothes faster than I can keep up with, and there's no way we can afford enough for him to eat if I'm begging on the corner again. Nasir warned me that he didn't have patience for mistakes, which just means that I won't make any.

The shouts and commotion were drawing closer, and Dan had just finished putting the final touches on the pomegranate display when he looked up to see a blur of red and brown streaking towards him. Jasper's crystal blue eyes were wide with panic as he ducked and wove his way under arms and around disgruntled shoppers. At a particularly congested spot, he leaped over a barrel of fish, impressively clearing the obstacle without knocking it over with his gangly legs. A pair of burly guards followed close behind him, delayed for a moment by the crowd of customers in front of the fishmonger's stand.

"DAN, WE'VE GOT TROUBLE!" Jasper's bellow was loud enough to draw the attention of everyone in the marketplace. Before Dan could form a response, Jasper had grabbed his wrist and pulled him forward with so much force that he was forced to drop the crate and run in order to avoid falling on his face.

"What's going on?" He pulled his arm free as they split to maneuver around a pair of women admiring a display of pottery. One of the women let out an exclamation of annoyance, shouting something rude after them, but Dan was already too far away to make sense of the words.

"No time to talk. Just run," Jasper answered between gasps of air. He rounded a corner, then immediately skidded to a stop. Dan, carried forward by momentum, had to jump to the side in order to avoid slamming into Jasper's back.

In front of them, a second pair of guards strolled up the street on patrol, their attention for the moment focused elsewhere. Dan glanced over his shoulder. The other guards, now red-faced and panting, were gaining ground quickly the further away from the congested marketplace they traveled. Without a second thought, Dan grabbed Jasper by the shoulder and pulled him into a narrow alleyway.

They ran through the cluttered alley, ducking under laundry hung stretched across from one wall to the other and skirting around piles of trash. The end of that alley led to another, and another, until finally they were on the other side of the marketplace. Dan led the way confidently, slipping between buildings, darting down side streets, and taking shortcuts that he was sure the guards had no idea of. They might patrol the streets of El-Huram, but Dan had grown up in them.

Worn and ragged tents replaced stone buildings, evidence that they had reached the poorest parts of town. The few structures that remained standing had long ago been abandoned and looted, and vacant, broken windows added an aura of hopelessness and desperation to the air. Children, shoeless and dirty, played a game of stickball in the street, calling out greetings to Jasper and Dan as they passed. Dan wound through the crowded slums until he came to their humble abode, an oilcloth tent stretched over posts that had been rummaged from the scaffolding of a construction site on the other side of town.

Jasper lifted the flap of the tent and threw himself unceremoniously onto the straw mat and pile of blankets that they called a bed. He closed his eyes with a groan. "This is the worst day ever."

Dan lowered himself cross-legged to the ground. "What's going on, Jas?" He did his best to keep his tone even and free of accusation.

I can kiss my job with Nasir goodbye after this. Even if I hadn't left in the middle of the workday, there's no way he missed the commotion that Jasper caused.

Jasper sat up slowly, brushing a shock of his buttery blonde hair out of his freckled face and stretching his legs out long in front of him. At twelve years old, he was already nearly as tall as Dan, with gangly arms and legs and a face that was stuck somewhere between a child and a young man.

"It wasn't my fault!" he insisted. "I didn't steal anything!"

"I never said you did," Dan responded patiently, even as his stomach dropped. He nervously fiddled with his mother's ring, spinning the smooth brass around his pinky. A charge of theft was no small matter in El-Huram these days, and, if convicted, the punishment would be severe.

Given the magistrate's attitude towards those citizens of El-Huram who called the slums their home, a conviction was almost guaranteed.

And given the magistrate's attitude towards Dan, it definitely was.

"I was just waiting to see if anyone had any work, like I do every morning," Jasper began. "I was going to go up to High Street because the folks are more likely to tip, but Malik got there first." He scowled at the mention of his competition, even though outside of work the two were friends. "So I went down to Market Street, thinking that maybe some of the sellers might have need of a courier today, seeing as how it's near the end of the month. I noticed that there was a new booth there at the corner of Market and Fountain, so I stopped to take a look. You've never seen such treasures, Dan! He had jeweled necklaces with gems as big as raisins, and little golden statues of pretty much every animal you can think of. And fancy lamps and goblets and plates and—"

"Jas, I don't need his whole inventory. What happened?"

"Right. Well, I just stopped to take a look and was moving along when I tripped over something in front of the table, and accidentally bumped into a lady next to me. She was looking at a necklace with the biggest ruby I've ever seen stuck in the middle of this golden sun thing. We both fell down and she dropped the necklace, but when I tried to give it back, part of the pendant was caught on the edge of my sleeve, and it wouldn't come off right away." Jasper held up his arm, showcasing the offending garment. A long, lonely thread hung down from the frayed edges of his faded red shirt. "She started yelling and accusing me of being a thief, and then the owner of the stall came over to see what all the trouble was about."

Dan rubbed tired hands over his eyes. "Did you explain to them what happened?"

"Of course I did! But she wouldn't listen, and neither did he. Then he called for the guards to come, which is when I dropped the necklace and ran."

"You left it there?"

"*Yes!*" Jasper crossed his arms with an offended huff. "I'm not a thief anymore."

"I know you're not. I just wanted to make sure I had all the facts straight." Dan exhaled long and slow as he thought through their next steps. Jasper's light, freckled skin and unique hair made him stand out in a city where almost every inhabitant had the same bronze-colored skin and dark hair, and there was little chance that the boy would go unrecognized. It would only be a matter of time before the guards found them again, and Dan wasn't about to leave his adopted brother alone to face the so-called justice of the magistrate.

Our best course of action is to go back to the merchant and try to explain things. The fact that Jasper left the necklace behind will hopefully be a mark in our favor. Hopefully the merchant will be reasonable.

"I'm sorry, Dan." Jasper's quiet voice was small and contrite. "I didn't mean to get us into trouble."

Dan shook his head. "It wasn't intentional. You panicked and ran, but you didn't actually do anything wrong."

"Are we going to get arrested?"

"No. Come on." Dan stood up and offered a hand to pull Jasper to his feet. "We'll go back and see if we can't smooth things over with...did you happen to catch the seller's name?"

"Vizriel."

"With Vizriel." Dan stepped out into the bright sunlight and blinked. "We'll get this all figured out, Jas. I promise."

They started retracing their steps to the marketplace but had gotten no further than a few blocks before being spotted by a patrolling guard.

"There they are!"

Within moments, Dan and Jasper were surrounded by four burly, scowling men, no doubt upset that they'd been given the slip once already. Strong hands gripped their arms, pulling them behind their backs, and the two young men were roughly marched down the streets until they came to Vizriel's booth.

It was even more impressive than Jasper had described. He had been so focused on the gold and jewels in his tale that he had neglected to describe the smooth finish of the mahogany posts, far too fine for a setting as mundane and ordinary as a market. Jasper had left out mention of the intricately woven fabrics that draped over the top and sides of the stall, forming a shelter from the blazing sun, that were more luxurious than even the tapestries in the magistrate's office. The dark blues, red, and purples of the fabric set off the precious metals and jewels on display to perfection, and Dan was not surprised to see that quite a crowd had gathered around Vizriel's stand. A short, balding man in ostentatious turquoise robes manned the stall, haggling with a customer over the price of a golden elephant statue with ruby eyes.

Jasper hissed a quiet curse.

"Jasper, language."

The boy rolled his eyes and cocked his head in the direction of the crowd. "He's here."

Dan's eyes followed the gesture to where two men stood to the side of the stand, deep in conversation, and his mind echoed Jasper's curse. The one standing closest to them, a middle-aged man in a blue brocade vest over his linen shirt, with gray streaks of hair at his temples and a close-cropped beard, was unfamiliar. Dan wished he could say the same of the second, a tall, imposing individual in dark robes who practically reeked of self-importance as he crossed his long arms over the thick chain that held the symbol of his position.

Chief Magistrate Hakim Ayad, the judge, jury, and executioner of El-Huram.

Dan swallowed the sudden nausea that accompanied his nerves. He had witnessed Hakim's particular brand of justice before as a mere bystander, and they were often bloody and gruesome enough to turn the stomachs of even the most hardened of criminals.

The problem was that it was the hardened criminals who padded Hakim's pockets, and therefore avoided his blade of justice.

"I'm going to die." Jasper's whimper was barely intelligible.

Dan gave his head a firm shake. "You're not going to die."

"This is Hakim. He doesn't like us. At the very least, I'll lose a hand, and then I might as well be dead."

Dan was cut off from responding by a hard shove between his shoulder blades. He stumbled forward, catching himself just before falling at Hakim's feet. In the corner of his eye, he saw that Jasper had not been quite as successful. The boy stood up slowly, wiping the dirt from his chin with his shoulder.

"We found the thief and his accomplice, Your Honor."

"I didn't have an accomplice," Jasper protested hotly. "And I'm not a thief! I didn't take anything."

Hakim looked down at them, the edges of his upper lip curling in disdain. Dan had been on the receiving end of the look countless times as a result of the magistrate's personal vendetta against him. Usually, he had his reputation as a hard and honest worker to protect him, though it did mean he was forced to bounce from job to job as employers saw him as a dangerous liability.

A sinking feeling in the pit of his stomach told him that his reputation would be of no use now.

Hakim directed his words at the man next to him. "Is this the culprit, Vizriel?"

Vizriel's eyes, bright with an unsettling interest, flicked over Dan and Jasper with the same assessing gaze he might give to an animal at auction. They focused for a moment on Dan's left hand and the ring on his finger. "The younger boy."

"But—" Dan's protest turned into a grunt of pain as he received a cuff to the side of his head.

"Where is it?" Hakim demanded. At a snap of his fingers, two of the guards had taken hold of Jasper's arms, holding him captive between them.

The boy's blue eyes blazed with defiance. "I told you! I didn't take anything!"

Hakim leaned in close, his voice low and dangerous. "You know the punishment for theft in El-Huram; don't add deception to your list of crimes."

Jasper paled but held his ground. "You can ask the lady who was there. The necklace got caught on my sleeve, but I didn't take it."

"That's not what Lady Fatima said."

Dan clenched his teeth in anger as understanding filled him. Whoever this Lady Fatima was, she must have seen Jasper as a convenient opportunity and pocketed the necklace for herself while directing the blame towards him. And because she was a member of the upper caste, Hakim would obviously believe her word over Jasper's.

"I didn't take it!"

Hakim leaned back, his expression turning bored. "Very well. Tariq? Your knife." He held out his hand and one of the guards behind Dan pulled a long, slightly curved blade from the sheath at his side. Hakim's long fingers wrapped around the handle, and he held it up. "You know the law, boy. The hand first, for the theft, then the tongue for the lie."

Jasper immediately started struggling against the guards' hold as Hakim advanced. Panic, cold and sharp, flooded Dan's veins, and he lunged forward, throwing an arm between Jasper and the knife. His shoulders were roughly seized in a vice-like grip, but he threw all his weight forward, straining to position himself in front of the magistrate.

"It was me! I'm the one who put him up to it." The lie was bitter on his tongue, but it had the desired effect. Hakim drew short, his blade stopping just above Dan's elbow.

"Ha! I knew he was nothing but a street rat!" Nasir's voice cut above the din of the crowd of spectators who had gathered to watch the meting out of justice. "You'll get no wages from me, boy."

Dan ground his teeth together and forced his face to remain stoic as he met the magistrate's cold, narrowed eyes.

"Dan..." Jasper's weak protest died away as he stared at the sharp metal edge. The weapon was polished until it shone, and it reflected the desert sun so brightly that looking at it hurt nearly as much as being cut open.

"You?" Hakim's voice bore just the slightest bit of surprise before something shifted in his face, and his lips spread into a slow, satisfied smile. "Well, it seems as if our incorruptible little *Aladdin* really does have a weakness, after all." He spat out Dan's full name, as if speaking the word left a foul taste in his mouth. "I knew it was only a matter of time before you were caught." He leaned forward to speak low into Dan's ear, carrying with him the smell of stale coffee and incense. "I must admit, I'm rather going to enjoy this."

Fear coiled like a tense spring in Dan's belly, but he held himself immoveable. His mind braced itself for the pain that he knew would be coming. He squeezed his eyes shut.

"I would like to propose an alternative."

Vizriel's voice, oily and dripping with opportunism, caused Dan's eyelids to fly open. The merchant was looking them over with a greedy, assessing gaze. His eyes flicked again and again to the ring on Dan's little finger. He crossed his arms in front of his chest, drawing Dan's attention for a moment to the gold thread that shimmered in the brocaded front of his vest.

Hakim scowled, no doubt annoyed at the delay. "The law is clear: the punishment for theft is loss of the offending limb."

"Unless the debt is repaid," Vizriel argued calmly.

A tiny flicker of hope flared to life in Dan's chest.

"Ha! And you think a couple of dirty street rats will be able to afford a jeweled necklace?" Hakim adjusted his grip on the knife.

The truth of his words snuffed out the tiny flame.

"Not with only one hand. They would both be far more valuable with two."

Hakim's brows lifted with wicked interest. "Continue."

"A man in my profession could always use a couple of strong lads. I think the two of them would come close to making up the value of the necklace that was lost."

The magistrate stroked his pointed beard thoughtfully and lowered his voice so that it would be indiscernible to the crowd. "The practice of slavery is illegal in Adhavi. If knowledge of this solution of yours became widely known, it could cost me my position."

Vizriel held up his hands as if to shield himself from the words. "Who said anything about slavery? All I'm proposing is an exchange of labor. You said yourself that they will never be able to pay off the sum of the necklace, and cutting off the boy's hand still leaves me out the value of the jewel."

Hakim's lips spread into a slow, understanding smile that reminded Dan of the crocodiles that lived along the riverbank. "I see. They will simply be working to pay off the debt."

"Precisely. I assume the boys have *some* marketable skills." He raised an eyebrow at Dan.

"My father was a tailor, and I learned from him," Dan answered quickly, seizing hold of the opportunity. "And I'm not afraid of hard work. Jasper has worked before as a courier and errand boy."

"Excellent. Omar!" Vizriel snapped his fingers at the turquoise-robed man behind the counter of his booth. "Keep an eye on things here. His Honor and I have some business to attend to."

Dan looked back and forth between the two men, certain that there must be a deeper meaning to what they were saying. It seemed too good to be true to believe that he would not only be allowed to retain full use of his limbs, but also ensure that he and Jasper would not be separated. But even if it took him years to pay off the necklace, he was much more likely to be able to secure employment again once the debt was paid if he didn't bear the mark of a thief.

A few years is a small price to pay if it means we still have a chance at a real future.

Two

Dan

Jasper kept up a steady stream of animated conversation as he and Dan shoved their few meager belongings into a burlap sack. "Do you think Vizriel will take us with him when he goes on his treasure hunts? Maybe I'll find something amazing!"

Dan wrapped one of the few books they owned in a threadbare blanket and motioned for Jasper to hold the mouth of the sack open wider. He gently dropped the bundle in, then reached for the very last thing—the leather case containing his father's fabric shears, a variety of needles, and a few spools of white and black thread. Though his family's tailor shop was little more than a pleasant, distant memory, he refused to give up the dream that someday he would be able to buy it back.

"I think we'll be spending a lot of time in Vizriel's company," he answered slowly, taking time to consider his words carefully. "But I wouldn't get my hopes up about being able to claim any treasure you find for yourself. Anything we find while working for Vizriel is going to belong to him."

Just like we do now.

Dan kept the bitter thought to himself as he stuffed a pouch containing their last few coins down into the bottom of the sack. When Hakim and Vizriel had presented him with the employment contract to sign, they had mistakenly assumed that he was as illiterate as Jasper, and so had not bothered to even hide the terms of the agreement. Vizriel claimed that the contract simply stated that Jasper and Dan would be obligated to work for him until such a time as the value of the stolen necklace was repaid in wages. What he left out was that the exact cost was never stated, which left it up to his own discretion, and that all living expenses—food, shelter, clothing—were to also be subtracted from their wages. This, combined with the fact that there was not a rate of payment enumerated at all in the document, meant that Vizriel had bought their futures with a jeweled necklace that may or may not have even been stolen in the first place.

Maybe it won't be so bad, Dan reasoned, searching for any possible bright spot. *Maybe he's actually quite generous and the contract was just to appease Hakim. He's had it out for me since the beginning. At the very least, life with Vizriel seems like it might be an adventure. He must travel all over Adhavi and beyond in order to find such marvelous things. Jasper will get to see the world, which is more than I could ever give him.*

Dan's eyes settled on the gangly youth as Jasper rolled up their straw mat and tucked it under his arm. He looked around the tent, empty now save for the makeshift table that they had fashioned out of a plank of wood and a couple of crates.

We're together, and we're whole, and that's all that matters for now.

"Alright, Jas, let's get going. Our future awaits."

It became evident very quickly over the following days why Vizriel had been so insistent that Dan and Jasper would be more valuable to him with their limbs fully intact. Like many of the other traveling merchants, Vizriel packed away his booth and merchandise at the end of each market day. All of the crates and supplies then had to be transported to the treasure hunter's camp on the outskirts of town. Though not an official part of any of the caravans that traveled to El-Huram on their trade routes, Dan learned that Vizriel was apparently well-known and respected enough among the traders to have earned himself their protection. In fact, so well regarded was Vizriel, that many of the merchants often remarked to Dan that his and Jasper's luck had changed for the better.

They did not know that Vizriel hid a cruel streak. He was strategic with his punishments, leaving bruises only where they could be covered up and choosing words and manipulation as his weapons more often than not. Dan tried to keep Jasper out of the line of fire as often as he could, but he couldn't always succeed. Thankfully, the boy's spirit remained undaunted, and he continued to regard their new life as something of an adventure.

"Dan! Did you hear?" Jasper was breathless and sweating when he arrived at their campsite shortly before sundown a week later. "Master Vizriel says that we're leaving in the morning. Do you think we're going to go on a real life treasure hunt?"

Dan looked up from where he sat near the campfire, mending the silk panels that hung from the booth. Once Vizriel had realized his proficiency with a needle and thread was not over-exaggerated, Dan frequently spent his evenings mending tears or replacing buttons. He didn't mind the work—as a tailor's son he had been sewing buttons almost as long as he had been walking—but it was difficult to keep the fabric clean amongst all the dust and sand of the desert that stretched out in nearly every direction beyond them. He pulled the panel out of the way just in time to avoid Jasper's dust-caked feet as he threw himself to the ground in an exhausted heap.

"I'm not sure how you think Master Vizriel finds his goods," Dan answered, an amused smile pulling at his face, "but I'm fairly certain he haggles, not hunts."

Jasper frowned. "But Omar said that Master Vizriel has traveled to the farthest corners of Adhavi to find his treasures," he argued, referencing the ostentatious fellow who helped man Vizriel's booth. "He's escaped booby traps and venomous creatures and even had to fight a band of forty thieves once!"

Dan set his work down for a moment and stretched out his stiff fingers. "I think Omar might be stretching the truth a little."

"Why?"

He shrugged. "People are a lot more likely to buy something if they think it has an interesting story behind it. Following clues to an ancient sultan's trove of hidden treasure is a lot more exciting than saying that Master Vizriel knows the right people to buy from along the trade route."

Jasper's face fell, and for a moment Dan regretted bursting his bubble of excitement. "Oh. So I guess the stories about the venomous snakes and the thieves probably aren't real, either."

"They might not be totally made up." Dan gave him a reassuring smile. "It's possible that Master Vizriel really did encounter some snakes or was attacked by thieves."

"I wish they were true. I've always wanted to go on an adventure and discover some real treasure. If we did, we would have enough money to buy a real house. And we could eat honey cakes every day!"

Dan chuckled as he picked up his needle and resumed his work. "I think you might get tired of them if you had them every day."

Jasper shook his head vehemently. "Not a chance. If I had a real treasure, I would have honey cakes at every meal. And I would buy clothes so you never had to make them again."

A hot, painful lump formed at the back of Dan's throat at Jasper's fervent words. "I like making your clothes. My father was a tailor, remember? I was going to run his shop with him."

"Then I'll buy you your tailor shop. You can be a businessman just like Master Vizriel, and I'll work for you making deliveries."

"I don't know," Dan said, pretending to contemplate the matter deeply. "If you eat honey cakes at every meal, you might get too slow to run around the city all day."

Jasper waved his hand dismissively. "That's easy. I'll just get a cart. I can make deliveries *while* eating honey cakes."

Dan laughed and ruffled the boy's hair. "You have a solution for everything, don't you? Very well. If we discover a treasure, I'll open a shop and you can be my delivery boy."

"Promise?" Jasper held out his pinky.

Dan linked his own pinky around it. "Promise."

Satisfied, Jasper jumped to his feet and began starting a cooking fire. "Do you think there will be camels? I've always wanted to ride one. Malik is going to be so jealous when he hears that I get to ride a camel."

Dan's thoughts drifted as the boy continued speculating about their upcoming adventure.

How do I break it to him that this is the only future we'll have? Vizriel practically owns us now. Honey cakes, a shop of our own—it's all just a fool's dream. Only one of Abba's miracles could make that happen, and you don't see a whole lot of those in the world.

Traveling by caravan was not nearly as glamorous or exciting as Jasper had hoped. The long line of camels carrying their heavy cargo moved slowly over the sand, and once they left El-Huram behind, the scenery changed little. Sand stretched out to the horizon on either side in smooth lines and gently rolling dunes, and it soon extended behind them as well. The silhouette of mountains in the distance ahead was the only notable landmark. It was to these mountains that the caravan was headed, but even after two days, they didn't seem to be any closer.

The novelty of traveling by camel was soon replaced by discomfort. Dan's legs and rear end were sore from riding the swaying beast, and every time he dismounted his muscles screamed in protest. He wore a long strip of fabric wrapped around his head and face, which, though it kept his skin from burning, made breathing a hot and stifling affair. His eyes ached from the unrelenting glare of the sun against the sparkling sand.

The caravan rolled to a slow stop at a small oasis at the end of their third day of travel. Dan went about his usual duties of feeding and watering the camels with enthusiasm, bolstered as he was by the idea of a swim and fresh, cool water to drink rather than the stale, tepid stuff they had been drinking since they departed El-Huram.

He was leading the camels to the edge of the water when Vizriel stopped him with a heavy hand on his shoulder. "Let Omar take care of the beasts," he said in a low voice. "Get the boy and come with me."

Dan's brows rose in surprise, but he did as his employer commanded. Jasper groaned when Dan pulled him up from the ground in front of the fire, but his attitude quickly shifted as he got caught up in the mystery.

"What does he want?"

"I don't know. He didn't say." Dan looked longingly toward the small pool of water that reflected the fading sunset and the palm trees that grew about it in small groves. "But I hope whatever it is, it can be accomplished quickly."

"I bet it has something to do with treasure!" Jasper's eyes sparkled with excitement. "Why else would he need us away from the others?"

Several reasons passed through Dan's mind, though none were very pleasant.

"Come with me," Vizriel commanded as soon as they reached him. He pressed a waterskin into Dan's chest as he turned and began walking towards a distant outcropping of rocks, adjusting the strap of the satchel over his shoulder as he went.

Dan immediately passed the water to Jasper, who tipped his head back and took long, deep gulps. "Where are we going?" He looked back over his shoulder at the campsite and the bright spots of cooking fires flickering in the growing darkness. With the sun dipping below the horizon, the air had grown cool, and Dan knew he would be thankful for the warmth of those fires before too long. The distant sounds of conversation and laughter carried over the sand. Their traveling companions were either unaware of or unbothered by their absence.

"Are we looking for a treasure?" Jasper asked eagerly, wiping droplets of water from his chin and passing the waterskin back to Dan. "Is it buried somewhere out here?"

Dan took a slow sip, relishing the cool liquid as it slid down his parched throat, but careful not to drink too much. Jasper would doubtless ask for more before the night was through.

Vizriel chuckled and ruffled Jasper's hair. The action set Dan on edge, though he knew better than to say anything and so held his tongue.

He hasn't done anything to make me suspect him of foul play...yet. But there's just something about this that doesn't sit right. What does he want from us?

"Something like that, my boy. There's a cave that's rumored to be hidden somewhere in those rocks ahead." Vizriel pointed with one of his jeweled fingers to the sharp outline that was just barely visible against the starry sky.

"What's in the cave?" Though Dan couldn't see Jasper's face, the breathless curiosity in his voice allowed Dan to easily picture his look of wide-eyed wonder.

Vizriel's voice dropped low, as if departing a sacred and secret knowledge. "If the stories are to be believed, treasure the likes of which you've never seen before—jewels and gold enough to make even the Sultan look like a beggar."

"Really?"

Dan was not as easily swayed by the mental picture of piles of wealth. "If that's the case, why haven't more people tried to find it?"

"Who says they haven't?" The merchant looked over his shoulder with a pointed expression. "But the cave is under a particular enchantment, and those who manage to escape alive do so empty-handed."

So what he's saying is that it's dangerous enough that he doesn't want to risk it himself.

"If that's the case, what makes you think that we'll succeed?"

"I have my reasons," Vizriel answered evasively. "Now come, we need to move faster if we're going to make it back before sunrise."

Tall rock formations loomed overhead as they drew near, and the soft sand under Dan's sandals began to be littered with loose stones. Vizriel threaded his way through narrow passages between the rocks, which in some places curved over them like the canopies used by the sellers in the marketplace and blocked their view of the starry sky. The moon was full, casting eerie shadows all about them, but Dan was grateful for the small amount of light as they traversed the uneven ground.

Finally, Vizriel came to a stop before a smooth rock face that towered twelve feet high. Up close, Dan could see the subtle striations of color in the stone that had been weathered smooth by sand and wind.

"Here," he said confidently, facing the wall of rock.

Dan glanced over at Jasper, who shared his look of incredulity as Vizriel dropped his satchel to the ground and began inspecting the rock, muttering under his breath the whole time.

"Are we supposed to climb?" Dan ventured carefully.

Instead of answering, Vizriel reached a hand into his robes and retrieved a small leather pouch. With his thumb and forefinger, he pulled out a pinch of some kind of sparkling dust, which he threw at the rock before replacing the pouch and holding both hands against the smooth surface. He began chanting strange words, and the low, ominous sound raised the hair at the back of Dan's neck.

After a few moments, the ground began to tremble. Jasper grabbed onto Dan's arm for support, and Dan reflexively pulled the boy close, throwing his other arm around Jasper's neck and head. The loose pebbles at their feet danced as, with a grinding, groaning sound, a dark hole opened up in the rock face before them.

Vizriel stepped back, a smile of smug satisfaction on his face. Dan's jaw dropped.

"It's a real secret treasure!" Jasper whooped, pushing away from Dan in his excitement. "With a hidden door and everything! But how did you know that it was there? I would never have guessed."

"I have my ways," their master responded mysteriously.

"Are we going to go in?" Jasper leaned forward eagerly, peering into the pitch-black hole.

"The cavern will only allow for one visitor at a time, and it must be one who is fairy-blessed."

The boy blinked up at him in confusion, his expression mirroring the swirling of Dan's thoughts. "But, how will you find someone?"

"I already have." Vizriel looked at Dan meaningfully.

"Me?" he asked, baffled. His face wrinkled. "I'm not blessed by anyone, let alone a fairy."

If I were, my parents wouldn't have died, and I wouldn't have been a beggar on the streets. I definitely wouldn't be little more than a slave now. If Abba has sent a fairy to bless me, it's not a very good one.

Vizriel's hand reached out, faster than a striking cobra, and grabbed hold of Dan's wrist. He held Dan's hand aloft. "Your ring. Where did you get it?"

"It—it was my mother's."

"She was blessed, then. The ring is a fairy mark. She gave it to you?" Vizriel's dark eyes were sharp and piercing.

"Yes, right before she died." Dan did his best to push the memories of that day from his mind. It was the day everything had changed—the last time he had a place and a family to call his own.

"We can only hope the blessing passed to him, then." Vizriel muttered the words quietly to himself before raising his voice. "I'm going to offer you a chance to change your life, Dan."

The tone in his voice was similar to the way he spoke to potential customers, trying to convince them that whatever he had for sale was absolutely necessary for their lives. Dan warily took the bait.

"What do you mean?"

"Down in that cave are enough riches to make even the Sultan look poor, and it's all yours for the taking. Just bring me the lamp that you'll find at the bottom, and the rest of the treasure is yours."

"You don't want it?"

Vizriel waved his hand, as if the mention of such glorious wealth was of little consequence to him. "Just bring me the lamp."

Dan looked at the dark doorway in the rock. He could just barely make out the edges of a few sandstone stairs in the cold moonlight, but after that the hole was dark and bottomless. He hesitated.

It's more than likely that Vizriel is sending me to my death, and that there really isn't the marvelous treasure that he claims. He probably is just using me as bait or to set off whatever traps lay inside.

He looked over at Jasper, taking in the young boy's excited eyes in the midst of his hungry, dirty face.

But what if he's telling the truth? With that kind of wealth, we could pay off whatever Vizriel claims we owe him. I could afford to actually give Jasper a home. He could have new clothes and go to school with the other boys his age. No more begging on the streets, and no more hungry nights.

"I can keep anything I find?" Dan forced his attention away from Jasper and back to Vizriel.

"Anything but the lamp," his master clarified. "Bring me that, and the rest is yours."

Dan took a deep breath and squared his shoulders. "Alright. I'll do it."

Vizriel rubbed his hands together with glee, his face lighting up with greedy excitement. "Excellent!" He pulled out a small bundle of tightly wrapped sticks from his satchel and gave it to Dan to hold while he lit the end with flint and steel.

With the torch held high in front of him, Dan approached the black, yawning door in the rock. Despite the warm, flickering light, he could barely see more than a few feet ahead. The darkness seemed to swallow and absorb the fire like a dry sponge in a bowl of water.

He glanced over his shoulder one last time at Jasper, then took the first step.

Nothing but empty air met the bottom of his foot.

Three

Dan

Panic, hot and sharp, flashed through him, and Dan yelped as he dropped the torch and threw himself backwards in an attempt to keep from pitching headlong into the darkness. He twisted, his hands searching wildly for something to hold onto. His fingers gripped the edge of the step and his feet scrambled for purchase but found nothing but smooth stone.

"Dan!" Jasper's voice was muffled and faint, as if it came from far away.

The darkness was heavy around him, and Dan felt a sensation as of someone taking his measure, weighing him to determine whether or not he was worthy. The ring on his finger burned hot, and he cried out in surprise, nearly losing his grip.

Then suddenly, the weight was gone, and solid ground appeared underneath his toes. Dan carefully checked over his straining shoulders before letting go of the edge above him. He was hanging above a small landing that ended in another set of stairs, wide and shallow, that descended a dozen feet under an arched doorway. The edges of the floor glowed with a warm, muted light, making the torch that lay burning at his feet completely unnecessary.

Dan carefully lowered his weight to his heels, recent experience leaving him distrustful of the reliability of the floor, and looked up. The edge of the steps was about three feet above him—far enough that he would need some assistance in getting out, but not such a long way that it would require more than a helping hand. Above it, he could still see the outline of the doorway and the velvety, starry sky outside.

"Dan!" Jasper's head appeared suddenly just outside the hole. "What happened? Are you alright?"

"I'm fine." Dan was still uncertain what exactly had just happened. There certainly seemed to be some kind of magic at work, but there was no need to cause the boy any more worry. "I just tripped."

"Did you find anything?" Now that he no longer was worried about Dan's safety, all of Jasper's previous excitement was bubbling back to the surface. "Is there really a treasure?"

"I can't tell. So far just a lot of stairs." Dan peered over his shoulder at the darkness behind him, narrowing his eyes and trying to get a better look at what lay beyond the archway at the bottom. "There's some kind of room down there, though."

"Go and see! And if there's a golden monkey, I want one."

Dan's heart rate had finally settled, and he was confident enough in the ground beneath his feet to allow himself to chuckle. "A golden monkey?"

"Like the elephant that Vizriel had—the one with the ruby eyes. But I want a monkey one. Or a tiger."

"I'll keep my eyes open."

"Good. Now go!"

With a smile on his face that only Jasper could bring, Dan bent down and retrieved the torch. Its light was redundant in the magical glow of the stairwell, but the flames were a comforting thought in case he should come across any other surprises.

Who knows what kind of creatures are living in a place like this.

The thought wiped the smile away from his face, and Dan gripped the torch a little tighter.

Abba, I could really use a little help down here.

He proceeded down the stairs, testing each step cautiously. The cave was as silent as a tomb, making the soft sound of Dan's footsteps and the breathing he was attempting to keep calm and controlled seem nearly deafening. He let out a sigh of relief when he reached the bottom of the stairs without mishap.

The cave was dark on the other side of the arched doorway, but as soon Dan passed the threshold, the room sprang to life. It brightened with the same warm glow that had illuminated his passage down, starting on either side of the door and spreading along the walls like a fire on the end of a fuse.

Dan's jaw dropped at the sight before him.

The ceiling of the room was high, nearly forty feet above him, and the room was larger than the entire marketplace of El-Huram. It was the contents of the room, however, rather than the size that drove all rational thought from his brain.

Piles of coins and jewels spilled and rolled like giant, glittering sand dunes across the room. Larger treasures—goblets, swords, the occasional shield or piece of armor—jutted from the piles at odd angles. A narrow pathway wound away from him and cut through the sea of gold and gems.

He walked along the sanded path, his sandals crunching over loose coins. The sound echoed against the hard walls, and a cold draft of air teased the ends of Dan's hair and made him shiver through his sweat-dampened shirt. Every curve of the path revealed something new, and he was obliged to admit that Vizriel had not been exaggerating when he said the treasure would make the Sultan's riches pale in comparison.

Finally, after what seemed like an endless, sparkling maze, Dan reached the other side of the room. An identical archway led into a long, narrow passage lined on either side with fruit trees laden with red and orange orbs. A sweet, fruity smell filled Dan's nostrils and his stomach immediately responded by growling, reminding him of the many long hours it had been since he had last eaten. He reached up to pluck a vibrant red pomegranate from the closest branch, then hesitated.

No. I can't get distracted. I promised to bring Vizriel the lamp, then I'll come back and get as much fruit as Jasper and I can carry.

With that bolstering thought, he pressed on.

After the fruit trees, a final door led him to a small, circular room. Unlike the others, this one had a tiled mosaic floor. Patterns of flowers in blue and yellow spread out from the center of the room, accented by swirls and leaves of polished jade. The walls were whitewashed and clean, and the magical light that had accompanied him thus far glowed with a softer, more welcoming light.

The room was completely empty, save for a lonely lampstand that stood in the center, highlighted by a single beam of moonlight that streamed in from above. Three legs of twisted iron, plain and unmemorable after the brilliance of the other rooms, joined together at the top to hold a small brass plate. A golden lamp balanced perfectly on top, its tarnished surface etched with delicate filigrees and set with red and purple gems around the flared base. A thin rounded handle on one side was balanced by a long, thin spout on the other.

This must be the lamp that Vizriel wants.

Dan approached the lampstand cautiously. It seemed strange that, with all the rest of the treasures available in the cave, an old lamp was the prize that his master desired.

Then again, it is rather hidden away. Maybe it's more valuable than it looks?

With shaking fingers, Dan lifted the lamp from its place, bracing himself for something horrible to happen when he did so. Warm magic brushed across the tips of his fingers, sending shivers up his arm, but otherwise the room remained quiet.

A relieved exhale escaped him, and Dan quickly turned around and began retracing his steps back to the entrance. It seemed to take less time than before to traverse the corridor through the trees and wide room of treasures, and before long he was climbing up the wide stairs.

"Hey, Jas!" he called when he came to the landing where he had fallen. "Come give me a hand?"

It was his master's form instead of Jasper's that appeared in the doorway, blocking out the starry sky. "Do you have the lamp?" Vizriel's voice was tight with excitement.

"Yes. Could you help me out?" Dan set the torch on the ground—he and Jasper would need it later when they went back down—and reached up a hand. His fingers just barely reached the edge of the ground above.

"Let me see!"

Dan held up the lamp, which was even more dull and dingy in the dim light.

Vizriel reached for it with trembling fingers. "At last." His words were little more than an exhale, but the desperate, slightly crazed expression that flashed across his face gave Dan an uneasy feeling in the pit of his stomach.

He pulled his hand back slightly, keeping the lamp just out of reach. "Where's Jasper?"

"Right here!" The boy's head appeared over Vizriel's shoulder.

"Give it to me." Vizriel's hand reached again for his prize. The gleam of crazed desire burned brighter in his eyes the longer he looked at the lamp.

It was then that Dan knew.

There's no way that he's going to let us have any of the treasure that remains. In fact, I would bet my mother's ring that he leaves us both in the desert in shallow graves as soon as he gets his hands on what he wants, though why a dusty old lamp is worth anything is beyond me. I need to find a way to get out of here and then distract him long enough that Jasper can get a good head start on running in the opposite direction.

"Help me up and I'll give it to you," he countered.

Vizriel's face twisted into a dark scowl of frustration. He screamed. "Give me the lamp!" In the blink of an eye, he had pulled Jasper from behind him and held a short, wicked-looking knife pressed against the boy's throat. "Give me the lamp," he repeated. "Or the boy dies."

Dan's heart stopped beating for a moment, and he froze. Jasper's eyes, wide and terrified, met his own. Vizriel's hand tightened around the handle of the knife, and a tiny drop of red appeared on the boy's neck. The treasure hunter wasn't bluffing; he was willing to kill in order to get his hands on the lamp.

What is this thing?

The metal handle suddenly felt hot in his hand, and Dan had the sudden urge to throw it as far away from him as he could. Instead, he willed his voice to remain calm and soothing. "I'll give it to you, Master Vizriel. Just let Jasper go. You don't have to hurt him."

"Hand it over first." Vizriel jostled his hostage a bit as he adjusted his hold and held out a waiting palm. Jasper whimpered as the blade nicked his skin again.

The sight and sound spurred Dan into action. "Here." He shoved the lamp into Vizriel's hand. "Now let him go."

Unfiltered glee washed over the treasure hunter's face as he beheld his prize. He crowed, "It's mine! It's finally mine!"

Dan kept his eyes glued on Jasper. "Which means you can let Jasper go now."

Vizriel tucked the lamp into a deep pocket of his robe with a nefarious chuckle. "Let him go? I'm afraid I can't let either of you go. Now that I have the lamp, I can't risk either of you squealing about its existence or trying to steal it for yourselves."

"But you said we could have any of the treasure we wanted!" Jasper's voice was indignant. "You said that if Dan got the lamp for you, we could have anything from the cave."

"And so you shall," Vizriel said, removing his blade from Jasper's throat and grabbing him by the back of his shirt. He shoved him towards the edge of the step. "You'll be able to keep the treasure for the rest of your life—however long that may be."

Having realized what his master was about to do, Jasper planted his feet and threw his weight backwards, resisting Vizriel's attempts to push him into the cave. In a move that Dan had seen him use several times before when dealing with bullies on the streets, Jasper ducked and dove to the side to dislodge Vizriel's grip on his shirt. He managed to succeed at first, but his foot caught on a loose stone and he tripped, landing on all fours.

Vizriel was on him before Jasper could scramble to his feet and start running. After a brief struggle, Vizriel sent him pitching headfirst into the cave with a mighty shove. Dan held out his arms, bracing himself to catch the gangly boy, who collided into his chest with enough force to knock the wind out of him and send them both crashing to the ground. The torch rolled away and bounced down the steps, knocking the flames out of existence.

As soon as Jasper's feet had passed the edge of the step, the rock above them began to groan with a deafening sound. The ground shook, the magical light blinked out, and the door to the outside slid shut, leaving them in pitch-black darkness.

Dan took a moment to collect himself as Jasper rolled to the side with a groan.

"That hurt."

"Is anything broken?" Dan sat up and gingerly felt the back of his head. A sizeable lump was already forming, but other than a few bruises on his back and ribs, he was otherwise unscathed.

"No. I'm fine."

An angry, bloodthirsty scream, loud enough to pierce the layers of rock above them, filled the air.

"Unlike that guy."

It was so dark that Dan couldn't even see his own hand in front of his face, but he could hear the smug grin in Jasper's voice. "Jas, what did you do?"

Jasper fumbled about for his hands before dropping something cold and metal into them. Dan carefully ran his fingers over the surface, feeling the rounded shape and the long, thin spout. A bark of laughter escaped him.

"I just figured that if the lamp was really so important," Jasper explained, "a person who was willing to kill innocents for it is the last person who should be allowed to have it."

"Under normal circumstances, I would probably scold you for returning to old habits, but I think I have to agree." Dan turned the lamp around in his hands, wondering again what it was that was so special about the piece of tarnished gold.

Vizriel obviously knows something, otherwise he wouldn't have gone to all that trouble to get it. But what?

"It also seems like a lamp would come in handy down here."

Jasper's innocent comment brought Dan crashing back to reality. They might have been able to take the lamp back from Vizriel, but they were still trapped inside the cave. They had no food, no water, and—based on the fact that there was not even a sliver of light anywhere to be seen—no way to get to the surface.

Or maybe there is one way...

The memory of the moonbeam in the lamp room gave Dan a flicker of hope.

"If only we had a way to light it," Dan answered ruefully, cautiously rising to his feet. He put out his hands, feeling for the wall. He kept one hand on the rough surface while turning his head in the direction he had last heard Jasper's voice. "As it is, we're going to have to do this blind. Do you trust me?"

Jasper's answer was swift and earnest. "You know I do."

"Take my hand and step carefully. This is going to take a while."

Step by tedious step, Dan led the way slowly down the stairs and through the treasure room, testing the space before each footfall. It was disorienting, traveling in complete darkness, and all sense of time and space soon became meaningless. It felt like years rather than hours or minutes before they finally reached the corridor with the fruit trees—a distinction only made by the suddenly sweet scents that filled the air. Dan stopped long enough to reach up and pluck a few of the fruits, stashing them away in his pockets for later.

They kept moving forward.

Jasper's breath hitched. "Is that light up ahead?"

Sure enough, a tiny spot of cold light beckoned to them across the distance of the corridor. The two hastened their steps, drawn to the light like moths to a flame and eager to leave the darkness behind.

The room was just as still and calm as before. The empty lampstand stood like a lonely sentinel in the middle of the floor. Dan rushed over and looked up, nearly weeping in relief at the small patch of sky visible through a chink in the ceiling.

His relief was short-lived, however. Dan and Jasper both scoured every inch of the walls, searching for any possible opening or means of escape, but the rounded walls were smooth and solid, and the only way out was through the door which they had entered. Dan slid down the wall to the floor in defeat, hugging his knees to his chest and resting his forehead against them. "I'm sorry, Jas."

"For what?" the boy scoffed as he fell to the ground beside him, long legs splayed out in front. "You're not the one who got us stuck in here. It's Vizriel's fault for being such a selfish, bloodthirsty villain." He paused for a moment. "Besides, I always thought it would be fun to have an adventure with a villain in it."

Dan turned his head to look at Jasper in disbelief. Despite their seemingly hopeless predicament, Jasper's expression was bright and unbothered. His blue eyes took in their surroundings with interest, as if they really were on some kind of adventure and not faced with a slow, tortuous death by thirst and starvation.

"It's not an adventure," Dan snapped. "We're trapped in this cave. We have no food, no water, and no way of getting out. The only person who knows we're in here wants us dead anyway, and if he were to rescue us, it would just be to kill us once he gets his hands on the lamp again."

Jasper was unfazed. "Vizriel isn't the only one who knows we're in here. The Abba knows. You're the one who always says that He will always look out for His children."

Dan sighed heavily. "You're right. I just don't know how exactly that's going to happen here." He leaned his head against the wall and closed his eyes, anxiously twisting the ring around his little finger. "I'm worried this is going to be the end for us."

"That's a pretty bleak outlook."

The unfamiliar and unexpected voice had Dan leaping to his feet and reaching for anything he could use as a weapon. He brandished the lamp above his head, then slowly lowered his arm as his brain registered the strange sight in front of him.

A short, grandmotherly figure stood in the center of the room. Her soft blue robes, wispy gray hair, and plump face all combined to give her an innocent, unassuming air, but her bright blue eyes were keen and sharp, and there was an air of authority behind her gaze.

"Who are you? Where did you come from? How did you get in here?" Dan immediately began looking around, seeking to identify her path of entry.

If she got in, then there must be a way to get out.

The mysterious woman laughed, a sound like tinkling bells. "So many questions, young Aladdin."

Dan froze. He turned to her again with wary eyes. "How do you know my name?"

"And there's another one," the woman said in a cheerful sing-song. "Perhaps if you waited to hear my answers to your first questions, the others would be answered."

Dan looked over at Jasper. The boy's eyes were bouncing back and forth between the two of them in wide delight. "You're his fairy guardian!"

"Oh, what a bright young man!" A wide, benevolent smile was turned Jasper's way, and he beamed at the praise like a puppy. "My name is Laelynn." She met Dan's gaze with a twinkle of amusement in her eyes. "I believe that answers your first and fourth questions."

"But—" Dan began to protest, before being silenced by Laelynn's hand.

"Let me finish, dear boy. As for your second and third questions, I came from my realm to this one when I was summoned by the ring." She nodded pointedly at the hand that still tightly clutched the lamp.

Dan blinked, trying to make sense of her words. "You're a fairy." Saying the words out loud made them sound even more ridiculous than they had been in his head. "My fairy guardian. And you came from another realm because of my mother's ring."

Laelynn clasped her hands together in front of her with a pleased expression. "Now you're catching on."

"But how?" Jasper interrupted. "I didn't hear him say any fancy words or do any of that chanting like Vizriel did outside the cave. One minute we were on our own and the next—*poof!*—there you were."

The fairy's expression turned dangerous for a moment. "Vizriel is meddling with magic that was never meant for humans. Of course Aladdin didn't need to do any of that. But the ring is fairy blessed, dear. If the wearer is in need, he must simply twist it around his finger three times and the need will be met."

Dan looked at her dubiously. "That doesn't seem right. I know for a fact that I've been in need many more times than this, and yet this is the first time I've seen you."

"I said your need would be met, not that I would appear. You really must learn to listen better to the answers when you ask questions."

A headache was beginning to form, and Dan closed his eyes and squeezed the bridge of his nose against the weight of what Laelynn was implying. He had neither the time nor the mental energy to sift through his memories of twisting his mother's ring to determine if a favorable outcome really had occurred soon after. Not when there were much more pressing issues to address.

"Can you get us out of here?" He dropped his hand back to his side.

Laelynn lifted one dark eyebrow.

"Please?"

She smiled. "As much as it would be my delight and pleasure, you really don't need me to do that. You already have all the tools at your disposal that you need."

Dan let out a frustrated scoff. "I don't know if you've looked around, but there is nothing down here." He threw his hands out to the side, gesturing to the empty room. "And since we can't just materialize out of thin air like you can, or eat that lampstand, we're going to die."

"Aren't there fruit trees?" Jasper interrupted, his attitude as sunny as Dan's was surly. "We won't starve."

Laelynn nodded sagely. "Indeed. Everything you need is already down here."

"If that's the case, then why are you here?" Dan leaned wearily against the wall. His body and mind were exhausted after a day of hot, hard travel, a late-night climb, and thwarting a crazed treasure hunter. And, underscoring it all, there was the voice in the back of his mind taunting him with the reality that the choice he had made in order to secure Jasper's future was the very thing that had put them into this predicament.

If I had just refused when Vizriel asked me to get the lamp...

"Because you needed a little bit of hope, dear." A warm hand rested on Dan's forearm, and he lifted his eyes to meet Laelynn's warm, sympathetic gaze.

"What is hope going to do for us? It's not going to magically make a door."

The fairy's lips tilted in a secret smile. "You'd be surprised. Hope is a powerful thing. Like the flame of a candle, it cuts through the darkness in the dead of night. And lucky for you," she added with a wink, "you have a lamp."

With those words, she disappeared like a puff of smoke. Dan just stared at the place on the floor where she had just been standing, halfway convinced that the fairy had just been a hallucination brought on by the stress of it all.

"I can't believe it! You have a real-life fairy guardian!" Jasper grabbed him by the shoulders and shook him excitedly. "A fairy!"

Dan shoved him away and sank to the ground, scrubbing a hand over his tired face. "Not that it does us a lot of good. We're still in the exact same place as we were before."

"But Laelynn said—"

"I know what she said!" Dan snapped, his words coming out harsher than he intended. "But unless this lamp can turn itself into a pickaxe, I don't see how it's going to get us out of here."

"Maybe there's something in the treasure room that can help us?" Jasper offered helpfully. His excitement had been unbridled when Dan had told him that the dark space they traversed on their journey really was full of gold and jewels. "We could go back and look."

"With what light? We have a lamp, but no way to start it. I don't even know why Vizriel thought it was so important in the first place." Dan held up the object of discussion in front of him, turning it from side to side to allow the moonlight to fall on all the tarnished spots. He gathered a corner of his sleeve and rubbed at one of the dulled marks. "It's just an old, dirty lamp."

The metal grew warm in his hands, and a stream of lavender smoke spilled out of the spout, pooling on the floor before rising in a tall, narrow pillar. After a few moments, the smoke cleared, and in its place stood a young woman. Her shiny black hair was pulled back into a thick braid, and brown eyes the color of coffee looked down at him disdainfully under dark brows. She crossed her arms over her chest, drawing attention to the golden bangles she wore in tall stacks on each wrist.

"Old and dirty? Have you looked in a mirror lately? You're not a sparkling diamond yourself."

Four

Aida

Aida kept her face aloof and unimpressed as she studied the two humans before her. She nearly laughed at the matching stunned expressions they wore—dropped jaws and wide, unblinking eyes. The younger of the two, still in his adolescent years, had the straw-colored hair and sky blue eyes of a Northerner. He was all gangly limbs and freckled skin, and the energy he exuded was rather like a young puppy. He clamped his jaw shut and bowed deeply at the waist, jabbing a bony elbow into the older one's side.

The older one—her new master, she surmised, as he was the one in possession of the lamp—was a bit slower to respond. His mouth closed, replaced by a guarded expression, and he pulled away from the wall, straightening his broad shoulders as he did so. He was only a few inches taller than her and, unlike his companion, he had the thick black hair and darker skin that was common in the desert. His hair held a slight wave and was sorely in need of a trim, swooping down over his forehead nearly to his eyes, which were a brown so dark that in the dim light they appeared black. His nose was straight, if a little wide, and his jawline sharp.

So she might have been bluffing a bit when she said he wasn't a sparkling diamond...but he really was dirty. Dirt and sweat streaked his handsome face, and his clothes were rumpled and smelled damp. Both of the humans wore attire more suited for peasants than the rich merchants and rulers she usually dealt with, though they were well-made and expertly tailored.

I suppose it makes sense that they wouldn't want to sully their fine clothes while crawling through caves in the desert, though I would have expected fewer patches.

"Dan!" the blonde one was whispering through clenched teeth as he again jabbed an elbow in the dark one's side. "Bow! Be polite."

The one called Dan gave the young puppy a look of exasperation before bowing stiffly at the waist, though not as deeply as his companion. "Are you a fairy, too?" His tone was as dry as the desert above.

The question, along with the rare showing of respect, broke Aida's control and distracted her from the rehearsed words she was about to deliver. She barked out a humorless laugh. "A fairy? Surely you know that's not the case, Master. After all, you're the one who summoned me."

Dan's face recoiled at her words, twisted in disgust and horror. "Master? I'm no one's master."

Aida tilted her head to the side and tapped her chin. She had experienced this reaction before—men who wanted to put her at ease and make her comfortable before making their true wishes known. It was best to let him know she was aware of exactly where she stood.

"Oh? But aren't you the one holding the lamp? Isn't that why you're here?"

Dan's head whipped around to face the blonde boy, and the two of them shared a look of horrified revulsion. "That's why Vizriel wanted the lamp," the young one said softly, his wide eyes looking from Dan to her. "He wanted her."

Aida crossed her arms again, clanking together the metal bracelets that never left her wrists. "Who's Vizriel?"

"He is—was—our employer," Dan explained slowly. "He's the one who wanted the lamp."

"If that's the case, why do you have it?" She sharpened her gaze. "Did you kill him?"

He wouldn't have been able to summon her if he had murdered the other man and taken it—the rules of the lamp would not allow for it. But there was something about the naive, shocked expressions on their faces that made her want to poke and prod. Something unusual was going on.

"What?"

"No!" Both humans reacted to her accusation with equal fervor. "But he was going to kill us," the young one explained. "He wanted Dan to get the lamp, and then when he brought it back, he was going to take it and leave us both behind to die in this cave."

"Which he still accomplished," Dan muttered darkly to himself.

The young one ignored him. "But I managed to steal it back from him before he pushed me, which is why he's out there without it and we're in here with you."

For the first time in many, many long years, Aida was surprised. "You had the lamp in your possession, and you just gave it to him?" She pointed to Dan.

"Yes? Why wouldn't I?" His brows pulled together in a puzzled expression. "For one thing, Dan was the one who was sent down to retrieve it, anyway. And for another, it seemed like it was important and he is much less likely to misplace it."

This is certainly a new one. Either the boy doesn't realize what it was he had, or he's being manipulated in some way.

"I'm surprised," Aida responded, raising her eyebrows in a calculated gesture. "Most men would never willingly give away such power. They would contrive a way to claim it for themselves."

"Power?" His freckled face wrinkled in confusion. "What kind of power?"

Ah, so the young one didn't know.

Aida glanced at Dan out of the corner of her eye, expecting him to react at any moment, commanding her not to say a word. When he did, of course, she would have to obey, but she could still plant the seed of doubt that would eventually grow between them. It would then be only a matter of time before they fought, one or both of them died, and she was left alone once more.

But instead of a furious warning, Dan was looking at her with just as confused an expression as the other one.

Oh, he's good. I'm almost convinced myself that he had no idea what he was doing.

"Yes, nearly unlimited magical power in the palm of your hand. The ability to grant almost any wish."

"But I thought you said you weren't a fairy."

There really was such a thing as dragging out an act too long. Aida, however, pushed down her annoyance and smiled sweetly at him. "I'm not. I'm a Genie."

The boy's eyes widened. "For real?" His words were an awed whisper. "First villains and then fairies and now Genies...this really is an adventure."

"Jasper," Dan sighed, pinching the bridge of his nose. He gave her an apologetic look. "I'm sorry..." He paused. "I don't know your name."

"Aida."

"Look, I'm sorry, Aida. Jasper tends to be a bit excitable. I'm sorry that we summoned you, or whatever happened, but now that you're here, would you mind helping us out? We're sort of trapped down here."

There it was. A twinge of disappointment twisted in her gut, though Dan had lasted quite a bit longer than her last masters before making demands. For just a brief moment, she had really been convinced that he might be different.

Though you shouldn't be surprised. They're all the same.

"Is that a command?" she asked woodenly.

"What? No! I mean, it's a request." Dan shoved his hand through his hair, pulling it away from his forehead before it fell down again, leaving him looking rather disheveled. "But if you can't, it's fine. I only thought that—"

"Can't?" Aida's temper flared to life. "Can't? You know very well that there is little I can't do here. After all, it's why you would have called me from my lamp in the first place. Now please, let's just drop this little charade where you pretend like you don't own me and my magic and just tell me what you want me to do."

Dan looked from her down to the lamp that he still held in his hands. His face paled, visible even in the dim moonlight. "Are you saying," he looked at her with a guilt-stricken face, "that as long as I'm holding the lamp, you have to do whatever I say?"

Aida rolled her eyes. "I didn't realize you were one of the ones who would want me to list it all out. Yes, Master. As long as the lamp is yours, I am yours to command. You have three wishes."

He didn't really. The binding magic hadn't imposed a limit, but Aida had discovered after the first few masters that the rules governing magical bargains seemed to overrule the ones that granted ownership of the lamp. As long as she could convince her human master to accept the bargain of three wishes, once the last one was spent, she would be left in peace for a while. It was helpful that humans generally seemed to expect hard and fast guidelines when it came to unfathomable power. Not a single one over the long centuries had questioned the three-wish rule.

"I can manipulate and change the natural world, but the spiritual is off-limits. I can't affect a person's soul. That also means that I can't alter other people's emotions or feelings against their will, I can't kill anyone for you, and I can't bring them back from the dead. I also can't manipulate magic itself, so don't think you can go around asking for magical powers. Other than that, your wish is my command." She finished her spiel and looked at him expectantly. "Now what is it you want me to do, Master?"

Dan looked at her in open-mouthed shock for a moment. He quickly shoved the lamp at her. "I'm not your master."

She laughed mirthlessly and pushed the lamp back towards him with the tips of her fingers. "You have the lamp. You summoned me. You're the Master now."

"But I don't want to be anyone's master." He pushed the lamp back in her direction. "You take it."

"That's not how this works." Aida's patience was growing thin. "*You* accepted the lamp. *You* rubbed the lamp. Why summon me if you don't want my power?"

"Because I didn't know that's what would happen!" Dan was on the edge of hysteria. "I was just trying to get rid of some of the tarnish. I certainly wouldn't have done that if I knew it meant you had to serve me. I didn't even know you existed."

Aida narrowed her eyes, trying to find any hint that would give away the fact that he was lying.

There was nothing but honest guilt and distress in his face.

"What if he wished for you to not have a master?"

She jumped at the sound of Jasper's voice. In her heated exchange with Dan, she had nearly forgotten that he was there. She gave him a wry look. "Weren't you listening during my explanation? I can't alter magic. Since magic is what binds me, there's nothing I can do to change that."

"There's really nothing we can do?" Dan twisted the lamp around in his hands. She had spent so long inside it this time that it was strange to see it from the outside. How many years of her life had been spent inside that tiny space?

The answer to that was easy: far too many to bother counting.

A thousand years of solitude broken only by selfish human after selfish human. They were all the same—power-hungry men and women who wanted riches and fame and would often stop at little to get it. The only reason she had gone so long between masters was because a fairy guardian had taken pity on her after the last one—she shivered to even picture his face—and granted her a safe place to hide away.

Oh well. All good things must come to an end, I suppose.

"Aida?" Dan's voice broke into her thoughts. "Is there really nothing we can do?"

She looked up at him in surprise. She had fully expected that he would sigh and make a show out of accepting his fate, and then settle in quickly to the idea of his wishes. Instead, he still seemed to be looking for a way to actively avoid them.

Aida thought she had seen it all when it came to the human race, but there were still apparently some surprises.

"Why does it bother you so much?" She tilted her head in thought as an idea slowly began forming at the back of her mind. Maybe this would really be her chance to break free—if not from the binding, at least from the incessant demands.

Dan looked at her as if she had two heads instead of one. "Because no person should ever be forced to do the will of another."

"I'm not a person."

He looked her up and down, blushing as he did so, and quickly met her eyes again. "You look like a person to me."

Aida held her arms out, considering her hands as she turned them back and forth. She looked down at her legs in the wide, yellow pants and the matching slippers on her feet. "I suppose so. But I'm not. I'm a Genie."

"So?"

She raised her eyebrows. "So do you even know what a Genie can do?" She snapped her fingers, suddenly filling the room with bright light. Dan and Jasper yelped in surprise and immediately shielded their eyes. Aida snapped again, and a long table appeared in the center of the floor, laden with a decadent feast and brilliant place settings that would be at home in any of the many palaces she had seen over the centuries.

Another snap, and instruments materialized out of thin air, filling the air with soulful melodies and luscious harmonies. Another, and Dan and Jasper were dressed in the finest clothes that money could buy, with jewels on their fingers and gold chains around their necks. An entire garden blinked into existence around them, with a bubbling fountain and sweet-smelling flowers.

"I could do animals, too," Aida said, resting her firsts on her hips. "But I don't like to just do it for show because it tends to scare the poor things." She twisted her hand, drawing her fingers in as if grabbing something out of the air, and everything disappeared again. With her hands again on her hips, she squared her shoulders and looked at Dan pointedly. "Still think I'm a person?"

"Yes." There was no hesitation in his answer, and Aida blinked in surprise. "But I think I can understand why you would be in danger from someone like Vizriel." He frowned. "There must be something we can do to help you."

Aida laughed at the absurdity of it all. "You want to help me? Aren't you the ones who are in need of my help?"

Dan blushed and looked down at his feet, mumbling something that Aida couldn't quite make out. Jasper jumped to his defense. "Laelynn said we already had every-thing we needed to get out of here, which means that we can help you get out, too."

The name rang a familiar bell. "Laelynn?"

"She's a fairy guardian—Dan's fairy guardian, as it turns out—and she told him that he already had all the tools he needed in order to get out of this place."

Aida let out a brittle laugh. Laelynn was the same fairy who had provided her the hidden sanctuary.

It appears she wasn't as kind and selfless as I thought. No doubt she was just keeping me somewhere safe until she could get me into her charge's hands.

She answered sardonically, "I think she meant that I was one of the tools."

Dan's head flew up at that. He set his jaw and shook his head stubbornly. "We'll find our own way out." He walked over and firmly placed the lamp back on the stand. "You can come with us, or you can stay here if you prefer."

He kept moving towards the darkness of the open door. "Come on, Jas. Maybe we can find something in the treasure room."

Jasper hurried past her, throwing a concerned look over his shoulder as he followed Dan from the room.

He really means it, at least for now. Maybe this actually could work.

"Wait."

Dan halted mid-step and turned on his heel at her words. He crossed his arms in front of his chest, drawing her attention to the muscles in his upper arms and shoulders. He was obviously not a stranger to hard labor, a fact that would hopefully work in her favor.

"What about an exchange?"

He raised an eyebrow in question. Jasper rocked back and forth on his heels, his eyes bouncing back and forth between the two of them as it had done before, glowing with something that looked like delight.

Aida cleared her throat. "I don't want to stay here."

"Like I said, you can come with us." Dan shrugged.

"I want you to take me to the palace."

"The palace? Why on earth would you want to go there?"

She hesitated, biting her lip. To divulge her reasoning now would mean baring her deepest desire to another soul—something that had not happened since before *his* treachery. With a deep breath, she explained, "I want to marry the prince."

Silence followed her announcement. Dan regarded her with narrowed, suspicious eyes. Jasper looked crestfallen.

"Why do you want to marry Prince Kamaran? How do you even know we have a prince?"

She lifted her chin haughtily. "I might be isolated here, but I'm not ignorant. I have a mirror that allows me to see any place in Adhavi and beyond. I've seen the palace, the Sultan, and Prince Kamaran several times."

"So you've been spying on him, and now you want to marry him? That might come across as a little...disconcerting."

"I've been watching," she argued with an exasperated growl. "It's not like I'm looking at him while he's sleeping or bathing or anything like that. But I've seen the way your human courts function, and I know that as his princess, I wouldn't have to listen to anyone. No one would be able to make demands of me; I would be making demands of them."

Dan was still for a moment, his brow drawn in thought. "You don't want to be a slave anymore."

The emotion that rose to the surface at hearing her wish spoken out loud was nearly too much to handle. She pressed her lips together and nodded curtly, not trusting herself to speak.

"But how will that work? What if someone finds out who you are?"

"You said yourself that I look like a person." Aida set her hands on her hips and gave him a challenging stare. "As long as you don't breathe a word about the lamp, there's no reason why they should ever know."

Dan looked over to Jasper, and something wordless seemed to pass between them. Aida's heart ached at the sight, remembering what it was like to be close enough to someone that no words were necessary for communication.

But her family was far away. None of them had been bothered to come looking for her, convinced by *him* of her untimely death. They hadn't even questioned, hadn't even bothered to verify the truth of his words. They had mourned her, of course, but life for them had moved on.

She had convinced herself to move on as well.

"What about the lamp?" Dan asked carefully.

Aida's arms shifted to a more protective pose, wrapping around her midsection. "What about it?"

"How does the...authority pass from person to person? Didn't you say that because I summoned you, I was the master? What happens if someone else takes it?"

"It only passes if the lamp is *given*. If it's stolen or picked up somewhere along the way, the magic doesn't bind me to my master's will. That's why it mattered that Jasper had given it to you. If you had taken it from him, it wouldn't have worked."

Dan ran a hand through his hair, his eyes unfocused as they stared at a spot on the floor while he contemplated her words. "So as long as I don't give the lamp away, you don't have to worry about someone else trying to control you."

Aida nodded. In truth, convincing Dan to keep the lamp was the element she was least concerned with. In her experience, humans were all too eager to latch onto her power and guard it with tight fists. Never once had they given the lamp away freely, unless, like Jasper, they were unaware of her and the magic they held.

No, the more difficult part of her plan would come once Dan got a taste of what her magic could really do for him. She didn't for a second think that she could trust him to allow her the freedom to live as she pleased, but there had to be some weakness of his she could exploit for her purposes—she just had to figure out what it was.

"Exactly. And I'll make it worth your trouble: you help me get to the palace and gain an audience with Prince Kamaran, and I'll still grant you your three wishes."

No human had yet been able to resist the offer of wishes, and Dan seemed to be no different. His eyes widened, and he looked over to Jasper for a moment. Aida could practically see the wheels in his mind spinning.

She was almost disappointed.

"What happens after the wishes are granted? Will you be sent back to the lamp? Will you still be able to use your magic if I'm not there to wish for things?"

Aida raised an impressed brow. She would have to be careful how she worded her answer, lest her new master get any new ideas. "I am bound to the lamp," she answered slowly. "But my magic is still my own. I must obey your *three*," she placed extra emphasis on the word, "wishes, but once they are done, I will simply return to being as I was before you summoned me: a Genie of the lamp. I don't have to stay in there." She motioned with her chin to her prison that Jasper held in his hands. "But there wasn't a lot of reason for me to come out of it down here in this cave."

"But how are you going to marry the prince?" Jasper interjected, his mouth pulling into a frown. "You're not a princess."

With a smirk, Aida held up her hand and snapped her fingers, picturing in her mind the exact image she wanted to present. Before her fingers had finished moving, she was covered from head to toe in patterned silk. The red skirt fell down to her toes in a long waterfall of smooth, shimmery fabric decorated with gold and white stitching. Tiny jewels embellished the floral pattern of the close-fitting bodice, and the capped sleeves were edged with gold ribbon. Rubies and sapphires glittered on her fingers, around her neck, and from the delicate tiara nestled into her intricately twisted and braided hair. The bangles at her wrists remained in place but shone with an extra polished gleam.

The cold air brushed over her bare arms, and, after a moment of thought, Aida added a contrasting gold scarf over her shoulders.

"I'm a princess now," she answered with a small shrug.

Jasper and Dan were both staring at her with mouths agape.

"A beautiful princess," Jasper whispered in awe. "Right, Dan?"

Dan's eyes flicked over her and then quickly returned to her face. Aida felt a small twinge of satisfaction at the blush that once again was filling his cheeks.

He swallowed thickly. "Yes." His voice cracked, and he cleared his throat. "You definitely look like a princess."

"So do we have a deal? You take me to Prince Kamaran, and I'll give you three wishes." Aida held out her hand as she had seen other humans do when sealing business negotiations.

Dan hesitated for a moment.

"Of course we have a deal!" Jasper exclaimed, grabbing Aida's hand himself.

A surprised laugh escaped her at the boy's enthusiasm, and she met Dan's eyes over his head.

He was looking at Jasper with a fond warmth in his gaze, which quickly strengthened into something more resolute. He gave her a sharp nod.

"We have a deal."

Five

Aida

Satisfaction and nerves swirled and danced in Aida's stomach at his words. It seemed too good to be true, too much like the fulfillment of her own wishes to really come to any fruition.

It's just as likely that he'll recover his senses and decide that he can't stand the thought of letting me out of his grip. But, at least for now, I suppose I might as well enjoy getting out of this cave and that lamp for a while.

The little flame of hope that had sparked eagerly to life refused to be put out, though Aida knew better than to allow it to grow.

She pulled her hand from Jasper's enthusiastic grip and took a step back. "Excellent."

"Does this mean we can get out of this cave now?" Jasper bounced lightly on the balls of his feet. "I didn't want to mention it before, but I kind of need to find a privy. Or a bush."

Dan groaned and pinched the bridge of his nose. "Jas, really? In front of a lady?"

The boy held his hands out wide. "What? It's true."

"That doesn't mean you need to say it."

Aida watched their exchange with a detached interest. She had been around the human race for too long to be surprised or disgusted by the mention of basic needs, and it was a little amusing to watch Dan squirm in embarrassment.

That amusement was all more welcome as it distracted her from the tiny thread of warmth that had tried to wrap itself around her heart when he called her a lady.

Her.

The Genie whose sole purpose to humans was to be used and then abandoned, whose value lay in what riches and power she could give them before she was either lost or stolen away and given to someone else.

She was the wish granter.

The money maker.

The instant ladder to the top.

But never a lady.

She cleared her throat and her mind along with it. This was no time to be distracted by fleeting sentiment. She had learned her lesson long ago—the less she allowed herself to feel for her human masters, the less it would hurt when she was abandoned, discarded, or ripped away in the end.

"We can leave any time you like. All I have to do is open the door." Aida raised her hand, her fingers poised to snap.

"Wait!" Dan lunged forward and grabbed her arm just below her bracelets. His hands were warm, and the skin was rough and calloused against her own.

She raised an eyebrow at him in question, and he quickly dropped her arm and backed up a few steps, sheepishly rubbing the back of his neck.

"Sorry. I just...what about Vizriel?"

"Who?"

"Our master, the one who sent me down here to find you. He wasn't too happy about the fact that Jasper and I got away. I wouldn't be surprised if he's out there watching the door, waiting for us to come out."

Aida shrugged. "I could make you strong enough to overpower him."

"I would really prefer to avoid violence, if at all possible," Dan answered with a grimace. "Vizriel had some kind of magic powder that he used to get the door open. Who knows what kind of tricks he'll have up his sleeve? I don't want to risk something happening to Jasper. Or to you."

"A sweet sentiment, I'm sure. But I can't just make us appear in the desert somewhere."

"I thought you could do almost anything," Jasper piped up. "Or were you just bluffing to get our attention?"

Aida glared at him with narrowed eyes. "I wasn't lying. But if we're not going to leave through the door, that means that I'll have to transport you by the Genie Ways, and I can't do that without a wish."

"Is it safe? For us humans, I mean?" Dan's arms were crossed again, and he rubbed his chin thoughtfully.

"As long as you stay with me, yes," Aida answered crisply. She really didn't understand the issue; one word, and she could easily make Dan strong enough to overpower a dozen men. In fact, most men would be drooling at the thought of such physical strength.

Jasper groaned. "Dan, you don't need to keep worrying about me. I could probably take Vizriel myself, if he wanted a fight. He might be bigger, but I'm scrappy." The boy made a show of flexing his muscles and hopping from foot to foot.

Dan ignored him. "And if we go this way, he'll have no way of knowing that you've left the cave?"

Aida squinted at him in confusion. "Why would that matter?"

"Because Vizriel is one of the only men out there who knows that you exist. He knows that we're trapped down here, which means that if we can leave without alerting him, he might not realize that you're gone."

Aida quickly filled in the missing pieces. "Ah. You're worried he might try to steal me away?"

"Aren't you? I've only known Vizriel for a few months, but I know enough to say that whatever he had planned for you, it didn't involve letting you anywhere out of his sight." Dan's face scrunched in disgust. "He definitely wouldn't want Prince Kamaran or any of the royal family to know about your existence."

"So your concern here is entirely for me?" Aida raised a skeptical brow. "It doesn't have anything to do with the fact that you won't get your wishes without me? That maybe having a Genie at your disposal is a little too tempting to just hand over?"

Dan threw his hands up with a frustrated groan. "Look, Ama—"

"Aida."

"Sorry. Aida. It's clear that you're going to believe whatever you want, regardless of what I say, but I don't want to be your master. What I do want is a way out of this cave that keeps both you and Jasper safe, so what do I need to say in order to make that happen?"

"This will count as one of your three wishes. I can't just give you this one for free because of your fancy words."

In truth, she could, if she wanted. Her magic was bound to his will, but not limited by it. And there was a tiny voice in the back of her mind that whispered that maybe, just maybe, this once she could take a chance and trust him.

But if I let him get away with it this time, it just sets a precedent that I can be won over with flattery and sentiment.

"I know." Dan held her gaze evenly. "What do I need to say?"

"Just wish for me to get us out of here unseen."

"That's it?"

"What were you expecting?"

He shrugged a shoulder. "I don't know. Maybe some fancy words or something."

"Nope. Just the words 'I wish' followed by your request."

Jasper cleared his throat. "Could you make it quick? It's kind of an emergency now."

Dan hesitated. "Do you really have to do anything I wish for? You can't say no?"

Aida could practically see the wheels turning in his mind, no doubt with the realization of what that might mean for him. She kept her face flat and her tone emotionless. "I am bound to serve the owner of the lamp."

He closed his eyes for a moment, drawing in a deep breath. Aida watched him closely, noting the way his hands clenched and unclenched into fists and his jaw tightened, causing a muscle under his left eye to twitch. He was obviously at war with himself about something.

Probably regretting the fact that his show of chivalry requires him to give up a wish.

Finally, Dan opened his eyes. He cleared his throat.

Here it comes. He's going to argue or try to find a way to work around the rules. They always do.

"I wish for you to get us out of here unseen, but only if it's something that you're willing to do."

Aida answered automatically. "Your wish is my..." She stopped mid-sentence as the magic that normally tightened around her chest and squeezed until she carried out the wish was held at bay. It was still there, but halted, as if waiting for something. The last of his words finally caught up to her. "...command? What did you say?"

"I said, I wish—"

She cut him off with a wave of her hand. "No, no. The last part. You added a condition." She drew her brows together in thought. No one, not in all of the thousand years she had been bound to her masters, had ever added a condition in her favor.

She didn't even know that such a thing was possible.

"I said I only wanted it if it was something you were willing to do."

"And if it's not?" she challenged him.

Dan shrugged. "Then you don't, and we find another way out."

"But the wish still counts. You will have wasted it."

He shrugged again, and when he held her gaze, his eyes were open and honest. "You're a person. You matter more than a wish, Aida."

A lump formed in the back of her throat at his words, and her eyes burned with unshed tears. Unable to say anything in response, Aida grabbed both of their hands, summoned a portal gate to the Genie Ways, and pulled them through.

"That was amazing!" Jasper's voice was filled with unmuted excitement as they stepped out of the Genie Ways and into the dry, hot air. "Can you really go anywhere in the world that way?"

Aida looked around them. The soft sand glittered in the early morning sun, and though it was still rather cool, the day promised to be a scorching one. To their right a small outcropping of rocks offered some shade, and she could hear the faint bubbling of a spring coming from somewhere among them. A few valiant green plants dotted the landscape, adding bits of color to the overall canvas of beige.

"I used to be able to," she answered quietly, her thoughts lost in a time long ago when she would spend hours daydreaming of all the places she would one day see. She blinked, clearing her thoughts. "Now I can only go where the owner of the lamp allows."

"That's still amazing, but I gotta go!" Jasper answered, glossing over her answer with a wave while he scrambled out of sight behind the rocks.

"What if I said you could go wherever you wanted?" Dan asked from behind her shoulder, startling her with his nearness.

She jumped and spun around, throwing her hands up in a defensive position.

Dan immediately stepped back, his hands open and placating. "I'm sorry!"

Aida slowly relaxed and lowered her arms. Dan mirrored her movement. "It's fine. I just didn't realize you were so close. To answer your question, it wouldn't really matter. The magical bond means that I can't be separated from the lamp for more than a day." Her chest squeezed with the reminder of the pain that resulted from her many attempts to run away in the beginning. She had served her first master long enough for him to grow lax with her leash, and at the first sign of freedom she bolted, only to be dragged back, panting and writhing, by the magic that tied her.

Dan pressed his lips together in thought, staring sightlessly at the ground in front of him. "That might make things difficult for the prince."

"How so?"

He blinked and turned his attention back to her face. In the bright light of day, Aida could clearly see the dark circles under his eyes and the shadowy patches of stubble that covered his cheeks. Weariness weighed down his shoulders.

"Because of your plan."

"My plan?" This close, she could see that Dan's eyes were not all one solid color, as they had seemed before. Instead, the warm brown was encircled with a ring the color of rich, dark chocolate. His full, undivided attention was on her, and it was hard to look away.

"To marry the prince? I can't imagine your husband would appreciate it very much if you had to visit some other man every day." His eyes flicked over her face, and his voice dropped to a whisper. "I know I wouldn't."

"Whew! I feel so much better now!" Jasper's voice cut through the strange tension that had been building between them. "Oh, sorry. Am I interrupting something?" There was a hopeful lilt to his voice.

"No!" Aida exclaimed, quickly pulling herself away. She cleared her throat. "Now that we're out of that cave, I think it would be a wonderful time to discuss the next steps."

"Does this mean we're going to go back to El-Huram?" Jasper bounded toward them with the eagerness of a puppy.

Dan shielded his eyes from the sun as he looked out over the sand in the direction of the royal city. "It certainly looks that way. But before we get started, we should move this conversation somewhere you won't burn to a crisp."

He led them to a shaded area between two large rocks. Jasper quickly climbed to the top of a low boulder, perching there like a bird in a nest. To her surprise, Dan rolled over another smaller stone.

"It's better than the ground," he explained, holding out a hand to help her sit.

She ignored both it and the persistent fluttering in her chest that accompanied the action.

It's nothing. He's just trying to flatter you and make you lower your guard. You've seen it before, Aida. Don't lose your head because a pair of kind eyes offered you a seat. He's your master, not your friend.

"We're not going to have to walk back, are we?" Jasper continued to chatter away, unaware of the storm of emotions brewing in her chest. "Can't we just use the magical stepping stones? That would be a lot easier. And there's not a chance of dying from thirst along the way. Do we even know how long it will take us to get home without camels?"

Dan leaned against the rock behind him, crossing his arms and legs at the ankle. "I think it would be best for us to avoid using Aida's travel techniques." He looked to her, as if seeking confirmation.

"It would cost you another wish," she conceded.

He shook his head. "That's not what I meant. It's only that, if you want Prince Kamaran—and the Sultan—to believe that you really are a visiting princess, you're going to have to let them see you approaching. If you just appear out of thin air, they're going to be suspicious and ask questions."

Aida tapped her chin as she considered his words. "I see. You're saying that I need to make an entrance. I need an entourage, attendants. Perhaps some sort of caravan? At the very least, I'll have to arrange some kind of transportation—"

Jasper leaned forward, nearly toppling from his position in his eagerness. "What about elephants? I've always wanted to see one up close, and I bet that would definitely get His Highness's attention."

"Jas, she doesn't need—" Dan started to protest.

"I like it!" Aida hopped to her feet and started pacing back and forth across the sand. The air had grown hotter, and with a flick of her fingers and hardly a thought, she summoned a cool breeze to wrap around her. "It will set me apart as someone foreign and pique Prince Kamaran's interest. And perhaps I should also make sure to bring a gift—gold and jewels and spices. Men in power seem to love those kinds of things." She gave a brittle laugh.

"How are you going to explain it all?"

Dan's question made her pause, and she lowered the fingers she had been about to snap and set everything in motion. "I already told you. I'll introduce myself as a foreign princess."

He shook his head. "But from what country? Where is it located? What are its exports or main trades? Even if you can get Prince Kamaran to fall in love with you, it's the Sultan you'll have to convince. How are you going to explain the fact that no one has ever heard of you?"

Aida frowned. She had not considered all the details that would be involved in her scheme. How was it that this scruffy, dirty servant knew which questions to ask?

"You seem to know quite a lot about it," she answered, resuming her seat and folding her hands in her lap.

"Dan's father was a tailor for the Sultan!" Jasper volunteered this information readily. "He got to go along to lots of fancy parties, and then he would tell Dan all about it. It's also why Dan knows how to sew better than most women."

"Thanks, Jas." Dan threw him a flat look, then turned to Aida with a shrug. "It's true, though. I don't know a lot about palace life, but I know enough to say that you'll need more of a story to be believable."

Aida suppressed a frustrated groan. Now that her dream was so close to becoming a reality, it was difficult to pull back and wait when all she wanted to do was rush ahead. "Fine, *Master*," she answered, spitting the word out with more bite than necessary and ignoring the way it made Dan flinch. "What do you want me to do?"

Six

Dan

Dan laced his fingers behind his head and stared up at the starry night sky. From somewhere behind him, he could hear the rustling sounds of Aida moving about in her tent. After a long, grueling afternoon of going over every angle of their plan and coming up with a believable backstory, it was decided that they would camp beside the rocks that night and make their entrance at the gates of El-Huram the following day. Once the decision was made, Aida immediately produced a tent for herself and disappeared inside, leaving Dan and Jasper to fend for themselves.

Jasper hadn't seemed to mind in the least, and the boy took a long drink from the little spring of water and immediately threw himself down onto the ground and fell asleep. The sound of his soft, even breaths lent a familiarity to the wide, unknown scenery that stretched around them on all sides.

Despite his exhaustion, Dan found himself unable to succumb to the same peaceful sleep that had so readily taken the boy. His thoughts swirled around his head, attempting to make sense of everything that had happened in the span of just a day. Magic, fairy guardians, Genies, wishes—all of it felt like he was suddenly thrust into one of the bedtime stories his mother would tell him by candlelight when he was a child. He had always wondered at how seriously his mother had taken the idea of fairies and magic; now he knew it was because she had known just how real it all was. The ring that she had given him on her deathbed—what he had assumed was simply a family heirloom—was fairy blessed. He had a fairy guardian.

Though I can't say she's been doing a very good job of guarding me so far, he thought morosely. *Or Jasper and I wouldn't have even been in the position we were in. We wouldn't have been reduced to begging on the streets or signed our lives away to Vizriel.*

He shifted, adjusting himself to a more comfortable position and nestling the lamp securely between his arm and side. At the movement, Jasper rolled over and faced him, resting his cheek on his arm and opening his eyes. The moonlight reflected off the white in his eyes.

"I thought you were asleep." Dan spoke the words softly, cognizant of the proximity of Aida's tent.

"I tried. But there's too much to think about."

Dan knew precisely how he felt.

"Can you believe it? I thought that fairy guardians and Genies and magic were all just a part of old stories." Jasper's voice was bright with excitement. "But it's real!"

"I suppose it makes sense. After all, there wouldn't be so many stories about them if there wasn't an element of truth."

"And you're always talking about how Abba is looking out for us. I bet that's why He sent Laelynn."

"Hmm." Dan still had more to think about before coming to a conclusion on that topic, though he could hear his mother's voice agreeing with Jasper.

"How do you think Aida got tied to the lamp?"

Jasper's question, innocently spoken, conjured an immediate, sick feeling in the pit of Dan's stomach. He recalled the dark, hollow look in Aida's striking eyes as she detailed his role as her master and her limitations. How often had she repeated those same words? How many cruel men like Vizriel had she been forced to serve? What kind of life was there to live within the confines of the tiny lamp?

He picked up the object in question and studied it as well as he could in the darkness. It seemed so completely unremarkable and unassuming, and yet it held Aida's past, present, and future captive.

He exhaled heavily. "I don't know. But I have a feeling it's not a pleasant story."

"Why would someone do something like that?"

"I would imagine for the same reason that humans do all other sorts of horrible things: money or power. Aida certainly seems to have the kind of power that could change someone's life." Dan thought back over the little display she had given in the cave. "There are a lot of men who would pay an extraordinary amount of money to be able to summon and control that kind of magic, and even those like Vizriel who would go so far as to commit murder to acquire it."

Jasper was quiet for a moment. "What are you going to use your wishes for?"

Dan returned the lamp to its place at his side and stared up at the stars. "I don't know. Honestly, I don't like the idea at all. I wonder if there's something we could do to free her."

"But your wishes are payment, right? We're taking her to the palace, and you get three wishes. But you should make the next one something better than your first wish. I can't believe you wasted one on just getting us out of the cave."

"That wasn't a waste. It got us all out of there safely."

"It was a boring wish."

Dan turned his head sideways and tilted his brows questioningly. "You think that whole experience was boring? Traveling by secret, magical roads wasn't interesting enough for you?"

"You know what I mean. If I had three wishes, I would wish for a house big enough for us and all of our friends in El-Huram. And a cake as big as a mountain. And maybe a tiger."

Dan chuckled. "A tiger, eh? And what exactly would you do with one?"

"Keep it as a pet," the boy answered promptly.

"Why not just find a cat?"

"Tigers are way more exciting. Plus, I bet no one would ever try to bother or cheat us if they knew we had a tiger. They're probably also really comfortable to cuddle with at night."

"I see. And the cake as big as a mountain? Why that particular wish?"

"Because I'm hungry." Jasper's stomach growled as if on cue, and he sat up. "Do you think Aida has anything to eat?" His head swiveled in the direction of Aida's tent.

"We're not going to bother her."

"Why not? It's not like it would even be hard for her. And it's not really fair that she has a tent and blankets to sleep in while we're out here with nothing." Jasper bent his legs underneath him, preparing to stand.

Dan's hand shot out and grabbed his shirt. "Jasper," he stated firmly, "leave her be."

"But I'm hungry."

"You've been hungry before."

They both had. Life on the streets meant they had often experienced the sharp pangs of hunger and the anxiety of not knowing where their next meal would come from.

"It's going to get cold."

"So we'll stick close together. We won't freeze."

Jasper's chin jutted out in a stubborn pout. He shoved Dan's hand away but made no further effort to rise. "I don't get it. She's a Genie. What's the harm in asking her for something to eat and a blanket? It's not like it would even cost her anything."

"You don't know that."

"She has magic. She snaps her fingers and things just appear."

Dan shook his head. "Some things come at a higher cost than money." His mind recalled the golden bracelets on Aida's wrists. Despite their exquisite craftsmanship and beauty, he hadn't missed the way they seemed to be fixed in place, reminding him more of shackles than fine jewelry. "The fact that Aida was bound to the lamp in the first place means that, at some point, someone decided she was worth more as a commodity than a person. How many other men and women like Vizriel have treated her as just an object, as a tool to get what they wanted?" His heart twisted with sympathy. "She's more than just her magic, and we're not going to ask her for anything, not when it won't cost us anything more than a little discomfort."

"I knew it! You like her." There was a smug satisfaction to Jasper's voice.

"What?" The question flew from his mouth louder and sharper than he had intended. The stirring in the tent behind them stalled for a moment, and Dan waited a moment before lowering his voice and continuing. "What in Adhavi gave you that idea?"

"She's beautiful."

The truth forced Dan to agree with Jasper's statement. "Well, yes; anyone could see that. But valuing her for her looks wouldn't be much different than valuing her for her magic." And while her beauty had certainly caught Dan by surprise when she first appeared, it was the strength and resilience of her spirit that he had seen glimpses of that intrigued him most. She had every excuse in the world to be sullen and jaded, and yet she was intent on reaching for her dreams and taking back control of the life that had been stolen from her.

"And you're taking care of her."

"I'm just making sure we don't take advantage of her situation. That's called being a decent human being. I take care of you all the time." Dan lifted himself onto his elbows and rolled his eyes in Jasper's direction, though it was unlikely the boy could see his expression.

"Not in this case," Jasper retorted with a deep, dramatic sigh. "She's warm and probably fed, and I'm still cold and hungry. What I wouldn't give for one Dalima's meat pies. Next time we follow our employer into the desert in the dark of night, we should pack some snacks. It's too bad the cave of treasures didn't have a fruit stand."

"The trees!" Dan sat up straight, suddenly recalling the fruit that he had plucked during their dark walk to the lamp room. "I picked some fruit while we were down there."

Jasper leaned forward eagerly. "Really? Why didn't you say something earlier?"

"Honestly? I forgot until just now." Dan reached a hand into his pocket, frowning as his fingers brushed against a hard, smooth surface and rigid lines. He slowly pulled it out, then held his palm up in an attempt to see the fruit more clearly. Moonlight reflected off a dark, multi-faceted surface. He laughed in disbelief as his mind registered the sight before him.

In the center of his palm lay a gem the size and shape of a small pomegranate. Dan quickly pulled a matching jewel from his other pocket.

"What's so funny? What are those?"

"I have some good news and some bad news, Jas. The bad news is that there isn't any fruit."

Jasper let out a disappointed whine.

"But the good news is that as soon as we get to El-Hu-ram, you can have as many of Delima's meat pies as you want."

Dan woke after a cold and restless night to a slippered toe in his side. Aida stood above him, looking like a vision from his dreams with the early morning sun behind her. He pressed the heels of his palms into his bleary eyes and yawned. "Good morning." Jasper shift-ed and rolled over beside him, muttering something in his sleep about camels.

Aida's brows were drawn together in confusion. "What are you doing on the ground?"

"I was sleeping." Dan stood and laced his fingers to-gether above his head and stretched from side to side. The stiff muscles in his back and neck protested the movement, and he grimaced. "Though I think I might be getting too old for camping under the stars."

He caught Aida watching him as he lowered his arms, but she quickly looked away, seeming to find a sudden fascination with the spot on the ground he had recently vacated. "You were there all night?"

Dan made a show of looking around. "Where else would we be?" Aida's own tent was gone; he imagined she must have dismissed it as she had done with all of the other objects she summoned.

I wonder where they all go? Do they just appear somewhere else? Or do they turn to dust and just stop existing anymore?

"But..." Aida was looking at him with a bewildered expression. "But you didn't say anything."

He shrugged. "It wasn't your problem to solve. I didn't want to bother you."

She studied him for a moment before understanding dawned. "You didn't want to use up your wishes."

"No, I—"

"What did you decide you want, then? Immeasurable wealth? Political influence? I can make you a prince, if you like. It wouldn't be surprising for you to arrive with me."

"Aida—"

"Or would you prefer something more subtle?" She tapped her chin with one long, perfectly manicured finger. "I could make you a learned sage. Those are the kinds of men who often are the real power behind the throne. We'll need to give you a beard or something, though." Dan blinked, and suddenly Aida was standing close, with her hands on his cheeks and the scent of oranges and jasmine filling his nose.

"Aid—"

"No one will believe you have words of wisdom with these patches of baby goat hair you have here." Her fingers trailed lightly over his jawline.

Dan reached up and captured her hands, holding them in place. "Aida." His voice was soft, but firm, and he waited for her to look him in the eyes.

She froze, suddenly, as if finally realizing how closely they stood, and her eyes widened as they slowly met his. A flash of fear, so fast he almost missed it, sparked in her gaze before her jaw flexed and she threw on a mask of confidence.

But he hadn't missed it, and Dan dropped her hands and took a step back, giving her space. "I don't want to be a prince or a sage, and I don't need immeasurable wealth." He gave her a teasing smile, attempting to inject some levity into the situation. "How would you even grant that wish? How do you know when wealth is no longer measurable?"

"When there's so much of it it's no longer worth the time or effort to measure."

"That seems rather arbitrary."

"It's flexible." Aida blew out a long breath as she fidgeted with her bracelets. Though each wrist had nearly a dozen stacked on top of each other, Dan realized that they never actually moved or jingled together when Aida moved her arms.

I wonder if she uses magic to accomplish that? And why?

"What do you want, then? Remember, I can't alter magic itself or affect the soul, so no love potions or magical powers."

Dan shoved his hands into his pockets, feeling the hard, glass-like surface of the gems. "I don't want anything."

Her face was a study in incredulity. "Nothing? I find that hard to believe. No offense, but aren't you both servants or something?"

His jaw clenched at the reminder. "We aren't servants."

Aida crossed her arms in challenge. "I thought you said you had a master. The man we were trying to avoid yesterday."

"We were working for him to repay a debt. He accused Jasper of stealing a necklace, and since it was his word against ours, the chief magistrate ruled against us. He was going to cut off Jasper's hand."

Her eyes flicked over to where the boy still lay sprawled out in sleep. "He looks like he still has all his limbs attached."

"Yes, because Vizriel offered to let us work for him in order to repay the debt."

"Aha! So you do need money."

"We don't."

"How else are you going to pay off your debt?"

Dan growled and pulled a hand through hair. "It should have already been paid!" Aida flinched at his harsh tone, and he immediately regretted it. "I'm sorry. I don't mean to yell. Vizriel has already gotten more than the value of the necklace in labor out of the two of us. I've seen the kinds of wares he sells, and believe me, they're not all as priceless and valuable as he tries to make people believe. But when he and Hakim put the contract together, they set the terms of compensation so low that Jasper and I will be working for years, if not a lifetime, to pay it off."

She looked unimpressed. "If you knew that, why did you sign it?"

"Because if I didn't, they would have taken Jasper's hand. Everyone in Adhavi knows a missing hand is the mark of a thief, and he would never be able to find work again. It wasn't just his hand, it was his future they would have taken." Dan's shoulders drooped. "And anyway, it turns out that what Vizriel really wanted was me and my ring in order to get into the cave. If he didn't get us that time, he would have found another way."

Aida nodded slowly at him as if having solved a mystery. "You're one of those types."

"What is that supposed to mean?"

"You like to play the hero. I bet you also make it your goal to take care of everyone and swoop in to save the day without a second thought."

Her words were like a slap across the face. Dan opened his mouth to respond, closed it, then opened it again. "I don't."

She tilted her head. "Oh, really? I wonder what Jasper would have to say about that? I don't suppose you stopped to ask him whether he preferred a life of servitude over a missing hand. Because I can tell you, having experienced one, I would take a stumpy arm with freedom any day." Her eyes flashed. "Now, what is your wish, master? Do you wish for me to erase the debt?"

Her words left him reeling. His mind was a storm of thoughts and emotions, and all he could do was stare at her blankly.

Is she right? Would Jasper really have been better off if I just left things alone? Did I—

"He doesn't need a wish to do that." Jasper's voice, groggy with sleep, caused them both to jump. "We're rich now. We're going to buy his shop and eat meat pies and honey cakes every day. Did you show her, Dan?"

Aida's eyes narrowed in suspicion. "Show me what?"

Dan pulled the fruit gems from his pockets. They were even more brilliant in the full light of day, a deep, ruby red color that seemed to glow from within. "We discovered that the trees in the cave aren't really fruit trees," he explained. "But, as you can see, the issue of money isn't really a problem right now. If Vizriel demands further payment, we can take care of it. I don't need wishes for that." He replaced the jewels. His mind was still spinning from Aida's words, but he pushed the thoughts away for later. "We have a busy day ahead of us. I'm going to get some water, and then you can tell us what we need to do to get you ready for Prince Kamaran."

A few hours later, Dan and Jasper were bringing up the rear of a grand procession. Musicians, camels and mules laden with spices, silk, and various treasures, a flock of peacocks, and even a tiger on a gold leash filled the wide street that led through the center of the city to the palace. Aida rode a camel near the front, looking every inch the princess she claimed to be in her luxurious dress and sparkling jewels. Her canopied saddle was open on the sides, giving the crowds that had gathered an unobstructed view of her regal, beautiful face. Dan could hear the whispered questions as they traveled from person to person, each trying to guess her identity.

"She must be royalty, to be dressed like that."

"She's here for Prince Kamaran, I have no doubt. I wonder what Lady Nadia is going to think of this. She's been the prince's favorite for a while."

"Did you see those jewels? Why, the rings on her hands alone could buy half the city!"

Dan tensed, looking warily to where a dozen figures in guard uniforms rode in front of Aida. To the unsuspecting eye, they appeared as real and human as he was. Only he, Jasper, and Aida knew the truth, which was that all of the guards, servants, and musicians were merely mannequins given the illusion of being alive. If any of the watching crowd were to decide to launch an attack, the guards would be completely useless. Aida would be on her own.

"She'll be fine," Jasper whispered from his place on Dan's right. They followed just far enough behind to seem like merely interested bystanders. "No one is going to risk attacking her this close to the palace."

Dan glanced over at him in surprise. "How did you know I was worried?"

"You get a wrinkle in your forehead here." Jasper pointed to the spot between his own eyebrows. "Usually it means that we're out of food or that we need more money for something, but it wasn't hard to guess this time, given the circumstances. Do you think she'll let me keep the tiger?" He looked up at Dan with the wide, hopeful eyes that had often gotten him out of trouble.

"Where would we keep a tiger? And how on earth would you feed it?"

"It can live above the shop. We'll feed it chicken."

Dan laughed. "I think keeping a tiger will require a little more than that. And we don't have the shop yet, anyway. They might not even be willing to sell."

"They will," Jasper answered confidently. "And then I'll get my tiger."

Dan was distracted as a lone heckler in the crowd raised his voice when Aida passed. "Hey, princess! I bet you would look even prettier if you smiled. Why don't you bring all those jewels over here and let me show you?"

His hands squeezed into fists, and he quickened his pace. As soon as the words left the heckler's mouth, Aida turned to him with an icy glare, sending the barest flick of her fingers his way. A pair of angry hornets appeared, buzzing around his head and stinging his lips and ears. He screamed in pain and batted them away as he fled. Aida smiled sweetly and waved after him.

Dan released the tension in his hands as Jasper caught up to him. "She's a little terrifying, isn't she?" the boy asked cheerfully.

"She is."

The procession had arrived at the gates of the palace, where one of her guards stepped forward and loudly announced her arrival. "Princess Aida Zorar of Jinnal, requests an audience with His Majesty, the Sultan, and brings gifts and offerings of goodwill."

The response from the palace guard was muffled, but the gates swung open slowly, allowing Aida and her retinue to pass through.

"And she's beautiful."

"Mmhmm." He barely registered Jasper's words, distracted as he was watching Aida disappear into the courtyard. So far, her plan was going just as she had hoped. Her words from earlier in the day replayed in his mind.

She said she would want freedom, not a hero.

"Just like my tiger will be."

Jasper's remark pulled Dan from his thoughts. He snorted a laugh and ruffled Jasper's hair before slinging an arm over his shoulders and turning the boy down a side street. "Let's not get ahead of ourselves. First we need to see a man about a shop."

Even if I made a mistake before, I'm going to make sure that Jasper has the future he deserves.

His free hand strayed to the bag at his side where Aida's lamp was safely tucked away.

And that Aida gets her freedom.

Seven

Aida

Aida's heart fluttered with anticipation and excitement as she took in the grandeur and decadence of the palace. Polished floors of intricately patterned mosaics, columns of white marble that led the eye up to curved ceilings just as beautifully tiled as the floors, hanging lamps dripping with crystals, gilded frames surrounding portraits of former rulers, woven tapestries on the walls—everywhere that she looked Aida found something new.

The palace guard led her down a hall that ended at two thick, golden doors nearly twenty feet high. They opened much easier than their size would suggest, and, after a whispered word from the guard to the herald, she was ushered through.

"Princess Aida Zorar of Jinnal."

White marble floors inlaid with tourmaline and lapis lazuli gleamed in the sunlight that streamed in through tall windows. A long rug in floral patterns of blue and silver with golden accents ran from the door to the raised dais between two wide pillars at the far end of the room. Three thrones sat atop it, two occupied and one empty.

She recognized the Sultan and Prince Kamaran immediately, their faces as familiar as her own after her many hours of observation in her magic mirror. The Sultan's long dark beard was streaked with gray, as was the hair around his temples. His keen eyes watched her with interest as she approached, and a smile appeared, barely visible under his beard. His long, cream-colored coat over his dark blue shirt and light trousers were casual and unassuming. Indeed, the only sign of his royal position lay in the ruby signet ring wrapped around his right index finger.

Prince Kamaran was a younger version of his father, but with gray eyes instead of brown and with a much shorter, neatly trimmed beard that emphasized the strong lines of his jaw and his high cheekbones. Where the Sultan's attire was understated and neutral, the prince appeared to embrace the concept of a royal wardrobe, with gold embroidery on his coat, mother of pearl buttons down the front of his black shirt, and a jeweled circlet around his head. He wore a ring on nearly every finger, which had been drumming in boredom on the arm of his throne until she stepped into the room. He straightened in surprise when he saw her.

Aida left her magical servants just inside the door in poses of polite anticipation and strode forward alone with confident steps and her chin held high. She had been around enough human royalty to know that one of the primary differences between them and their subjects was the expectation of deference.

If I want them to treat me like a princess, I have to act like I am owed it.

She stopped just before the dais and bent her knees in a polite curtsey as she gave the rulers her most winning smile.

"Princess Aida, this is a most unexpected surprise." The Sultan tilted his head slightly as he studied her. "Both in that we had no warning of your impending arrival, and in that Jinnal is not a country I can claim to be familiar with." There was an edge of suspicion to his tone, though his eyes and the smile he gave her remained warm.

Aida clasped her hands in front of her, tamping down the panic that threatened to turn her stomach into a swarm of anxious bees.

I already anticipated this line of questioning. I just need to stick to the story that we came up with yesterday.

She shifted her smile to one of apology and gave a sheepish shrug to her shoulders. "Ah, yes. I must beg your pardon for the unannounced arrival, Your Majesty. Jinnal is not a large country, and though we are not lacking in natural resources, our people are a far more limited com-modity. It was simply more prudent for us to send myself along in lieu of a messenger. But though you have not heard of Jinnal, I can assure you that Adhavi is well-known to us." Aida flicked her eyes over to Prince Kamaran before looking down at her hands with a shy smile. She smoothed the skirts of her gold and turquoise dress. She had chosen the color specifically to subtly match the throne room, sending the subliminal message that perhaps she belonged there.

As she had intended, neither the Sultan nor Prince Kamaran missed the subtle action. A pleased smirk pulled at Kamaran's lips, and his father nodded in understanding.

"I see. Well, despite the surprise, we are certainly delighted to have you."

"Your hospitality is too kind. And as a show of both appreciation and goodwill, please allow me to present these gifts from Jinnal." Aida beckoned towards the servants at the door, and they moved forward, bearing baskets and trays laden with spices, exotic fruits, fine fabrics, and other treasures. Her new master had been an invaluable resource in advising her what sort of gifts might best be received.

The Sultan's eyes widened as he took in the costly goods before him, and Prince Kamaran was so excited he rose to his feet to get a better view. Aida smiled widely. As a Genie, materials such as gold and precious gems meant little to her, able as she was to simply summon them at will, but it never ceased to amaze her just how pliable the sight of such things made humans.

"This is indeed a lovely and generous gift." Prince Kamaran stepped lightly down the steps to stand before her. He reached for her hand and pressed a kiss to the back of it. "But the princess who accompanies it is lovelier still."

Aida did her best not to squirm at the butterflies that erupted in her stomach as the prince tucked her hand into the crook of his arm and turned to the Sultan. "Father, with your permission, I will escort Princess Aida to a set of rooms. I'm sure she must be exhausted after a journey across the desert."

"Of course. And see to it that her people are taken care of as well."

Aida shook her head. "If it's all the same to Your Majesty, my people are all perfectly capable of finding lodging for themselves in town. I will admit that your city holds quite the reputation, and they are eager to experience El-Huram for themselves."

A slight frown creased the Sultan's brow. "Are you certain?"

"Of course." Aida laid her free hand on Prince Kamaran's arm just above his elbow. "I feel quite safe here. There is no need for an additional strain on your resources."

He studied her for a long moment before finally nodding. "As you wish. If you are feeling refreshed, we would be honored if you joined us for dinner this evening."

Aida smiled her thanks and allowed Prince Kamaran to lead her from the room. She sent her magic into the mannequin guards as she passed, directing them to leave the palace before disappearing into thin air.

Prince Kamaran guided her down several lavish hallways and through a quiet garden before entering a smaller, more private wing of the palace.

"Here we are," he announced with a flourish, causing his rings to sparkle as they caught the light. "These rooms will be yours for the duration of your stay, which I hope will be a long one."

Aida let go of his arm and stepped into the spacious sitting room, turning in a slow circle as she took in the beautiful furnishings. The room was decorated in deep jewel tones, soft whites and creams, and dark wooden accents. Layers of curtains hung over a patio door, though they had been tied back to allow a view of the verdant gardens beyond. Aida could hear the distant trickling of a fountain.

A low table and a long settee were arranged in the middle of the room, along with a pile of soft cushions and pillows that had been scattered over the floor for sitting or reclining.

"This is lovely," Aida breathed in admiration.

Prince Kamaran moved to stand beside her, clasping his hands behind his back. He smiled at her reaction. "I'm pleased it meets with your approval. I'm sure it must be much different from the accommodations you are accustomed to, at least if the sampling of Jinnal goods in the throne room is any indication."

Yes, certainly different than what I'm used to. I've lived in a lamp for the last thousand years.

"It's perfect, Your Highness. I couldn't ask for a lovelier place to stay."

"Please, call me Kamaran. I find titles to be wearisome when speaking among friends."

Aida raised her brow, giving him a flirtatious smile. "Are we friends, then?"

"I certainly would like to be."

Aida inwardly squealed at his ready concession. *So far, this is going even better than I had hoped.*

Kamaran nodded towards a door to their left. "The bedroom and washroom are just through there, and there is an adjacent chamber if you would like to keep your maid close by."

"Oh." Aida looked down with a demure chuckle and willed a soft blush to suffuse her cheeks. "I didn't bring a maid with me. I knew traveling the desert would be taxing, and I am more than capable of taking care of myself."

"I can see that." Kamaran's eyes looked her up and down appreciatively. "Still, there's no need for you to do that here. You're our guest, and a princess. These hands shouldn't be forced to do such menial tasks." He pulled the fingertips of both her hands and pressed them to his lips, maintaining eye contact with her the whole time. "I'll make sure someone is assigned to take care of you."

The intense, focused way he was looking at her was rather overwhelming, and Aida's butterflies turned into little bundles of nerves. "Thank you," she responded breathlessly, pulling her hands free. "I would appreciate that."

"Of course, Aida. Will you allow me to escort you to dinner this evening? I would love to hear all about Jinnal and get to know you better."

"That would be wonderful," Aida forced the words out with a smile, despite the sudden feeling that perhaps his focused attention wouldn't be.

No. This whole plan revolves around securing his interest. If that means suffering through a dinner fielding questions about my imaginary country, then so be it. Besides, it's better to do it now when the answers are all fresh in my brain.

"I look forward to it." With a bow and a flourish, Kamaran backed out of her door, leaving her alone for the first time in two days.

Her solitude, as well as her misgivings about her plan, were short-lived. Not more than a quarter of an hour passed before a knock at the door revealed a small army of maids and attendants, all eager to wait on her every whim.

Aida sighed in contentment as she leaned her head against the side of the large, deep bath as one of the young girls—Aida was fairly certain her name was Samira—combed some sort of sweet-smelling oil through her hair. Rose petals floated on the surface of the steaming water, enveloping her in their soft, floral scent. One of the other maids had already laid out one of the dresses from the trunk she had the foresight to summon, and the others had gone in and out, bringing hot water for the bath and a tray of tea, fruit, and cheese for refreshment. They had since left to return to their other duties, leaving Samira as her sole companion.

"Your hair is beautiful, Your Highness."

It took Aida several seconds to realize that the title belonged to her. "Oh—ah...thank you." She cringed inwardly at her own awkwardness.

Samira didn't appear to take notice of it at all. "It's so long and thick, and the comb just slides right through it. When I do my sisters' hair, it's always like fighting my way through a rat's nest."

Aida blinked, unsure what to do in the situation. She'd had female friends as a child, before the lamp. But it had been centuries since she had spoken with anyone on such a mundane subject as...hair. And certainly not with such familiarity. She wasn't entirely certain she could remember how to carry on a conversation.

Samira kept chatting as she worked. "It probably doesn't help that they spend all day outside in the sun and wind. It tends to dry the hair out, you know? I have to give them an oil treatment every week, and it still is just barely manageable."

"Do you have many sisters?" Aida finally ventured when Samira paused to take a breath. It seemed like a safe enough question.

"There are five of us. Yasmin is the oldest; she works in the kitchen with the pastry chef, which is a handy connection to have. I'm next, and then the triplets—Dalia, Nadia, and Zaria. I'm not quite sure why my father and mother thought it was a good idea to give them such similar names. I suppose matching names for a matching set seemed like a good idea at the time, but I'm always calling them the wrong name, and I'm their sister. No one else stands a chance. Most everyone else just calls them the Ia's. They work with Mother in the gardens."

Aida's mind was spinning under the deluge of information, and she grasped at the first thing she could. "Does your whole family work at the palace, then?"

"Yes. Father is one of the heralds, which Mother says is the perfect job for him because he has such a big voice and he loves talking." Samira giggled. "Mother also says it's a family trait."

A huff of laughter escaped Aida. "I can see that."

"Oh!" Samira's ministrations suddenly stopped. "I'm speaking too much, aren't I? I'm so sorry, Your Highness. Mother also says that I don't know how to leave a moment of silence unfilled. But I won't be offended if you tell me it's too much."

Aida shook her head, slowly speaking the words as she sorted through her thoughts. "No, it's fine. I don't really mind. I'm just...not very good at this. At talking, I mean."

She wasn't sure what exactly had possessed her to divulge the information. As a rule, she did everything she could to keep her vulnerabilities hidden. Perhaps it was the open, friendly way that Samira included her in the conversation, as if she expected they would be friends for some time. Or maybe it was the fact that, for the first time in a thousand years, she wasn't conversing with someone who held power over her. Either way, she couldn't deny the part of her that wanted, desperately, for Samira to continue to talk to her.

To include her in the conversation like she was just another one of her girl friends.

Like she wasn't a Genie trapped in a bottle.

Like she was free.

"Oh, that's all right," Samira reassured her with another laugh. "I can talk enough for both of us. Now, I heard that you're supposed to accompany Prince Kamaran to dinner. Is there anything you want to know about El-Huram or the royal family before then? I can't promise to know the answers to all your questions, but I have lived here all my eighteen years of life, so I know a bit."

Aida bit her lip, considering what she really wanted to know. "What can you tell me about Prince Kamaran?"

Eight

Aida

True to her word, Samira regaled Aida with nearly every story or fact she could remember about Adhavi's crown prince. Aida learned that Kamaran, though he was heir to the throne, had a reputation for being a bit indolent. He often shirked his duties in favor of attending social events or participating in recreational duties with his friends, and there were some in El-Huram especially who questioned his suitability to rule when the time came.

He was also known for being something of a flirt, and, according to Samira, his unmarried status had everything to do with his inability to settle his attentions on one woman.

"Although if anyone was capable of catching his eye, I think it would be you," Samira offered with an encouraging pat on the shoulder as she put the finishing touches on Aida's hair. "You have a little bit of this mysterious, otherworldly quality that I bet most men find irresistible.

Not to mention you seem smart enough to handle his mischief and keep him in line. There. What do you think?" She gave the hair a final tug and stepped back, allowing Aida to survey herself in the mirror.

She turned her head back and forth, examining Samira's work. Her hair was curled and twisted in a fancy updo that had taken the girl nearly an hour to complete. Aida ignored the fact that she could have done it herself in less than a second with her magic. The time spent with Samira had been enjoyable.

And very informative.

She smiled into the mirror, meeting Samira's eyes. She had the kind of understated beauty that would only continue to grow with age, made all the more attractive by the sparkle of good humor in her eyes. She was short, coming barely to Aida's shoulders, but her personality filled the entire room.

"It looks lovely, Samira."

"Really?" Samira clasped her hands in front of her chest. "I've always wanted to try something like this, but none of my sisters are patient enough. You're a very good sitter." She gave Aida a wide smile.

You learn a lot of patience sitting in a lamp, waiting for your next master to show up.

"It's one of my many strengths."

"Oooh! And a dry wit, too! Prince Kamaran won't stand a chance against you."

By the time dinner was done, Aida began to wish that Samira's prediction had been false. From the moment she left her room, Kamaran was glued to her side, paying her lavish compliments, anticipating her every need, and peppering her with questions about her homeland. He was particularly interested in the economy and trade, and expressed several times how impressed he was that such a country so rich in natural resources and precious goods could have gone so long unnoticed.

When the meal was over, Kamaran made a show of introducing her to all the important visitors and guests, drawing attention to her beauty and status but never letting her get in a word edgewise. Though he was all charming smiles and smooth compliments, Aida felt like an ornament on his arm, or a lovely piece of art meant to be admired and coveted rather than a real person. As the night wore on, the attention and noise began to grate on her nerves, which were far more accustomed to silence and solitude.

She took her leave at the earliest opportunity, claiming fatigue from her long journey, and escaped to her rooms where the moonlit gardens under her balcony beckoned with their sweet smells and soothing silence. Aida wandered along the paths, enjoying the feel of the cool night breeze on her face after the stuffy air indoors.

A dull ache, just under her ribs, caught her attention. It felt as if a string were tied to the bone and someone on the other end was tugging at it, urging her to follow.

The lamp.

Guilt mixed with an edge of panic soured her stomach. She had been so focused on gaining entry to the palace that, once they had entered the city gates, Aida had completely disregarded Dan and Jasper.

They could be anywhere in this city. We never settled on a time or place for them to meet. I don't even know where they planned to go. She pressed a hand to her side and grimaced at the thought of the pain that was sure to come. *Though I suppose I'll find out soon enough.*

"Psst, Aida!"

She jumped at the sound of her name, whirling around to find the source. Her wanderings had taken her to the corner of the garden closest to the outside wall, and a hand beckoned to her from behind a tall hedge. Aida stepped cautiously over, keeping her hands raised and ready to strike if necessary.

Dan's face peeked around the corner of the shrubbery, followed by Jasper's a little lower. "It's just us."

Aida immediately relaxed, and she felt the tension of the phantom string lessen the closer she moved to them. "What are you doing here? How did you get in?" From what she could recall of the layout of the palace, the garden was not only behind the main walls, but tucked away so that it was surrounded by buildings and guards on all sides.

Jasper waggled his eyebrows. "I'm a man of many skills."

Dan rolled his eyes. "I don't know about the 'man' part, but he has a knack for finding his way in and out of places. One that he doesn't use anymore—" He turned towards the boy and widened his eyes meaningfully as he emphasized each word. "—unless it's truly necessary."

Aida crossed her arms in an effort to ward off both the chill in the air and the strange feeling of relief that accompanied their arrival. She kept her voice toneless and detached. "And it was necessary to sneak into the Sultan's garden?"

He must be here for his wishes. I knew it would only be a matter of time before he realized what he was missing. Well, I at least got an afternoon of freedom out of the deal. Though I wouldn't have complained if he had come to this realization before dinner.

Dan's expression changed to one of uncertainty. "Yes?" He shared a glance with Jasper before fixing her with his full attention. "Did you say that you couldn't be separated from the lamp for very long?"

"I did. But that still doesn't answer my question." She shivered slightly as a cool brush of air whispered over her bare shoulders.

"You had no way of knowing where we were. At least, I assumed you didn't. Maybe I was wrong? Does your magic let you locate the lamp?" Dan shrugged out of his jacket and held it out to her.

Aida simply stared at it. "What's that for?"

"You're cold." He gave it a tiny shake, indicating that she should take it.

"He's being a gentleman," Jasper added in a stage whisper. "It's what a man does when he's trying to impress a woman."

Dan closed his eyes and inhaled deeply through his nose, as if summoning a final reserve of patience. He gave Jasper a flat look. "Or when you're just trying to be kind."

Trying to be kind? Or just trying to throw me off my guard? He's my master, not my friend.

Aida said nothing, but held Dan's gaze while she snapped her fingers, summoning a wrap around her shoulders that contrasted perfectly with her dress.

His cheeks flushed with embarrassment, and he slowly retracted his arm, hanging his jacket over his forearm rather than putting it on.

Guilt gnawed again at Aida's insides, but she tamped it down.

I've seen this game before. I won't fall for the caring, chivalrous act.

Dan cleared his throat. "Anyway. If you were able to find the lamp after all, I apologize for interrupting your night. We'll let you have your solitude again." He turned to leave.

The tamping wasn't working against the dejected slump of his shoulders. Aida found her voice. "Dan, wait."

It was the first time she had said his name out loud, and the word seemed to sparkle with its own kind of magic as it hung in the air.

He and Jasper both looked over their shoulders.

"I...I didn't know where the lamp was. At least, not yet. I would have been able to find it when the time limit wore off, whether I liked it or not, but the experience is always quite unpleasant."

Dan turned fully around. "What do you mean?"

Aida carefully surveyed their surroundings. She was fairly confident that they were alone, but nothing good would come of anyone finding out who and what she really was.

"The binding. It's like a rope tied around my wrists and chest. When I've been gone for too long, it pulls and squeezes until I don't have a choice but to follow."

He had moved closer to her as she was speaking and was just an arm's length away. His eyes, soft with compassion, roved over her face. "I'm sorry, Aida."

His tone was warm and gentle, and she wanted nothing else but to close her eyes and let it wash over her like a hug. But doing so would mean letting her guard down and admitting that she cared even a little about him, so instead she responded with an indifferent shrug. "It's not your fault."

"But that doesn't mean I'm not sorry that someone did this to you."

A crack in the hard shell around her heart formed, and Aida responded in panic. She curled her lips into a sneer. "I don't want your pity. And I don't need your heroics, either. I'm sure you didn't just come all this way to tell me how sorry you are for me. What's your second wish?"

Dan studied her for a moment longer, his expression unreadable. After a few long seconds, he threw his jacket over one shoulder and shoved his other hand in his pocket. "I don't pity you, Aida," he said quietly. A sad smile formed on his face. "Jasper and I are at the tailor's shop on Bayid street. It's not far from the palace; you should be able to find it easily. You are free to come and go as you like."

He turned on his heel and followed Jasper into the darkness, doubtless needing to sneak out the same way they had gotten in. She stared after them, her eyes unfocused as she worked to process the myriad of emotions swirling in her chest.

Dan's spoken permission, though Aida was certain he was unaware, had loosened something inside her. It was the sensation of suddenly being able to breathe clean air for the first time after being confined to a small, stuffy space. The bonds that tied her to the lamp were still there—she could feel the warm, raised skin of the angry red scars that wrapped around her wrists underneath her bracelets—but the leash was longer. She had been given a tiny taste of freedom, and it was intoxicating.

And the thought that it could so suddenly be stripped away was terrifying.

Which is why I need to get Prince Kamaran to marry me. Once I'm a princess, I'll have the freedom to do whatever I want.

"What about Dan?" a voice in the back of her mind protested. *"What happens when his wishes are used up? Not even marriage to a prince can save you from the lamp. Another master will come, and you'll be just as trapped as you were before."*

"He wouldn't get rid of me," Aida whispered into the darkness. "He wants to be a hero too much for that. And if it's money that he wants, I'll be a princess. I can give him any price he wants for keeping the lamp to himself."

The spark of hope, stubborn and resilient, flared to life again in her chest, only to be once again quelled by her inner voice.

That's a lot of trust that you're putting in one man. You know where that got you the last time.

"But maybe this time it will be different."

Though she said the words, Aida could not find it in herself to believe them.

After all, she was a Genie.

She knew far too much about wishful thinking.

Nine

Dan

"DAN!" Jasper's yell rang through the small shop a few weeks later, completely overpowering the cheerful tinkling of the bell above the door as it slammed open.

Dan started, stabbing himself with his needle in the process. He sighed and set aside the pair of trousers he had been mending, careful not to let any of the blood that was starting to drip from his finger touch the expensive fabric. "Back here, Jas."

He heard Jasper coming around the counter in the front and then his head appeared in the doorway of the small workroom. His face was flushed and sweaty, and he breathed heavily as he leaned over and rested his hands on his knees.

"Were you running?" Dan stood and stretched his back, which was sore from bending over his work all morning, before searching the pile of fabric scraps for something to tie around his bleeding finger. The workroom was a study in organized chaos, with bolts of fabric stacked on shelves from floor to ceiling. One wall held a unit with tiny cubbies and drawers full of buttons, clasps, ribbons, and spools of thread in every color imaginable. Aida's lamp was hidden away in the corner of one of the shelves, surrounded by other containers and bowls that kept it from looking out of place. A clothing rack held projects in various stages of completion, and a pile of previously worn and discarded clothes stood nearly waist-high on the worn wooden floor, leaving only a narrow path between the dunes of clothes for Dan to walk from the door to his workbench.

"Hakim is here."

Dan's head flew up at the words, and the bandage he had been tying fell to the floor.

"I mean, not *here* here, but I saw him over on Aliba street. I was stopping to get a honey cake after my delivery like you said I could, and he was coming out of the jeweler's next door."

Dan bent down to retrieve the bandage, taking a deep breath to calm his racing heart. "Hakim is the chief magistrate of El-Huram, and he probably lives in this part of the city. It makes sense that you would see him around."

"But I didn't just see him. He saw me. And then he stared, and his face turned a kind of reddish purple."

"Did he say anything?"

"I don't know. He was with another man I didn't recognize, and when he turned to ask him a question, I ran."

Dan pinched the bridge of his nose. "Jas, running makes it seem like you have something to hide."

"But I don't!" The boy stood up straight now, his eyes wide and wounded.

"I know that. And you know that. But you know Hakim has never liked us." Dan dropped his hand, fiddling with his ring as he did so. A sour feeling pooled in the bottom of his stomach. "He could cause a lot of trouble for us if he wanted to. He knows about our contract with Vizriel."

Jasper huffed. "Which wasn't very legal. What?" he asked when Dan blinked in surprise. "You think I'm not paying attention, but I hear things. I know Vizriel was practically trying to make us slaves."

"You knew? But you acted the whole time like it was going to be some kind of grand adventure."

"We did get a chance to leave the city for a while." The boy shrugged. "And I really did think we might get to go on a treasure hunt. Besides, we were together, and that's what mattered."

Aida's words that had haunted him since their conversation in the desert weeks before played through his mind. "Do you blame me?"

Jasper looked at him like he had grown a second head. "For what?"

"For putting you in that situation. For taking away your freedom. I didn't ask what you wanted; I just jumped in and made the decision for you."

"There wasn't exactly time for us to have a conversation about it. We both know that Hakim was out for blood, one way or another. I didn't really feel like having my hand cut off that day. Besides, I knew that you would find some way to get us out of it; you always do." Jasper grinned wide-ly. "Though I didn't expect you to find a Genie."

Dan exhaled a quiet laugh in relief and amusement. "I can honestly say I wasn't expecting it, either." A warm, tingly feeling filled his chest as it did whenever he thought of Aida. Since her introduction to the prince a few weeks before, she had been a daily visitor to their little tailor shop. Though she had been uncertain at first, Aida had quickly become a comfortable fixture. When she came, she sat in the workroom, talking and laughing with Jasper or watching with fascination as Dan worked. She still held herself aloof and distant, but slowly and surely her hard exterior was beginning to crack, and she was starting to trust them. Dan knew that, with her history, it would take a while for her to believe that they truly cared about her, but he had hope that eventually she would see that she had nothing to fear from them.

His mind jumped to a conversation that had hap-pened just the previous week.

Aida was later in coming than usual, caught up as she was with some social activity with Prince Kamaran, and Jasper had long since retreated to their apartment above the shop. The soft glow of a candle lit the workroom as he labored over the jacket he was mending and resizing.

The soft click of the lock alerted him to Aida's presence; with her magic, he never had to worry about leaving her a key. Her cheeks were flushed and her eyes were red, as if she had been crying, when she entered the workroom. "You're still here?" Her question sounded more like a statement, and her shoulders had dropped just the tiniest bit with relief.

"I thought it would be more comfortable for you to come here than upstairs," he answered, searching her face. Something was obviously troubling her. "Are you alright?"

She pressed her lips together and cleared her face of emotion. "I'm fine," she said primly. "I appreciate you waiting."

"It was no trouble." He gave her one last, long look before turning back to his work. "I had some extra projects to keep me busy."

Silence fell over the room, broken only by the soft, pulling sound of his thread through the fabric. It was the first time since the desert that they had been together without Jasper as a buffer, and an uncertain tension stretched between them.

"What are you working on?" Aida finally asked.

Dan held up the jacket. "Something for one of Jasper's old friends. Malik has an interview tomorrow with a shopkeeper, and he wants to make a good impression."

"For working in a shop?" She stepped into the room and leaned over the workbench to get a closer look. Her refreshing scent of jasmine and citrus filled his senses, and Dan had to keep himself from leaning in and inhaling deeply.

"It's much better than standing on the corner and begging for work as a courier, which is what Malik's presently doing." Dan forced himself to focus on his task, and not on the beautiful woman standing over him.

Aida's fingers appeared in his field of vision, brushing against his hand as she rubbed. "This is expensive wool," she stated. "How is his friend able to afford this if he's been begging?" Her hand retreated. "Did he steal it?"

"What? No!" Dan quickly straightened. "I have a whole collection of cast-offs from clients. Sometimes they ask for a bit of payment for them, but usually they're just trying to get rid of things that are too small or too worn for them to use again."

Aida crossed her arms and canted her head. She looked at him consideringly. "And do you do this sort of thing often?"

He shrugged self-consciously. "A little. We used to live in the slums, Jasper and I. I know what it's like to always have to worry about finding clothes that fit or how to replace pieces that were ruined. And it's something that my father and mother used to do, back when they owned the place. It seemed fitting that we take it up again."

Aida looked back and forth between him and the pile of used clothing on the floor. "It seems like a lot of work."

"It is."

"You could just wish for me to do it for you."

Dan's heart ached for her. Aida was constantly looking for ways that he could—or would—use her. Even after so much time in his presence, she still refused to believe that his only interest in her lamp was in order to keep her safe. It made his efforts to find any information he could on removing the magical binding even more important.

"No. The work is part of what makes it special."

"What do you mean?"

"Most of the folks living in the slums deal every day with either the pity or disdain of those in better situations. They are seen and treated as lesser citizens, not as equals, or as people worth knowing and caring about. I put time and effort into their clothes because I want them to know that they

are worthy of it. By caring about their clothes, I'm caring about them."

"That's...nice." The words were spoken almost condescendingly, but Dan had looked up and seen the wheels turning behind the mask of indifference she wore. And suddenly, inspiration flashed.

He knew a way to make Aida see that she was more than just a Genie in a lamp.

"What are you smiling about?"

He looked up to see Aida regarding him with a mixture of suspicion and curiosity. His smile faltered a little at the reminder that she was still so guarded around them. He pushed his idea to the side for a moment.

"Nothing important right now." He paused, then held out the jacket. "Do you want to help?"

"Help? Like with the needle?" Her beautiful face was twisted in confusion.

He nodded.

"But I don't know how."

Dan stood and patted his empty seat. "I can show you."

Aida sank hesitantly into the chair, and he handed her the jacket and needle. "We'll start with something simple, like reattaching this button. Hold it in one hand like this, and the needle in the other." He leaned over her shoulder and wrapped his hand around her, gently adjusting her grip so that she wouldn't stab her fingers as she pushed the needle through. Jasmine and citrus filled his nose, and he blinked, forcing his mind to focus on the task. "Use the button holes as your guides. Start from the bottom, come up through one hole and go down through another."

Aida's brow pulled together as she focused on her task, using slow, meticulous movements. When Dan declared her work satisfactory, she looked up at him with bright, excited eyes.

"I did it!"

Her smile was wide and beaming with contagious joy. His position at her shoulder meant that their faces were only a few inches apart, and he could see the flecks of gold in her deep, chocolate eyes.

"You're thinking about her, aren't you?" Jasper's sing-song, teasing voice pulled him from his memory.

Dan's face heated, and he lied. "I wasn't."

"You were." Jasper leaned against the doorframe and crossed his arms and legs, looking even longer and lankier than normal. "You get this goofy smile on your face and your eyes get all mushy. You liiiiiike her." He laughed and ducked as Dan threw a balled up piece of fabric at his head.

Dan sighed. Denying it further would only encourage Jasper's already blatant match-making attempts. "She's amazing."

"I knew it!" Jasper pumped a fist in the air. "So what's the plan? Woo her slowly? Sweep her off her feet?"

"First of all, sweep her off her feet? It makes it sound like you're pulling a rug out from under her." He shook his head in wry amusement. "Second, where are these ideas even coming from?"

"Malik has younger sisters that like to read romance stories." Jasper's freckled face wrinkled with disgust. "But coming back to the topic at hand, what is your move?"

"I don't have a move."

"Obviously. Otherwise she wouldn't be trying to marry the prince."

Jealousy, hot and uncomfortable, writhed in his gut. "Don't remind me."

"If it bothers you, do something!"

Dan dropped his face into his hands before pulling at the ends of his hair. "It's not that simple."

"Why? You said yourself she was amazing. And she's certainly beautiful enough."

"Aida's more than beautiful. She's smart and witty and strong and resilient. She's been through so much, and yet she still has a desire to make a better life. And though she tries to hide it, she cares about others. She's far kinder to humans than she needs to be, and far more merciful than many might be, given her situation."

"What do you mean?"

"You've seen what she can do, Jas."

"Yes, and? She has rules that she has to follow."

Dan leaned back in his chair. "I've been thinking about that. Other than tying her to me, the lamp doesn't seem to have suppressed her magical abilities. All of those things she did to make a good first impression on the Sultan? I didn't wish for any of them, which means that she still has some measure of free will. I think that's what she meant when she said her magic was still her own. She can still use her magic in any way she pleases, and if she wanted, she could make life miserable for a lot of people. Remember the hornets? But she doesn't."

Jasper looked thoughtful. "That's a good thing, though, right?"

"Oh, definitely. But if you think about the fact that Aida has been bound to the lamp and forced to serve humans for what must feel like an eternity, the fact that she doesn't just exact her revenge on us all at every available moment is quite telling. I've known washerwomen who were more vindictive over less."

"She probably knows that you would just force her to go back into the lamp and wait if she acted out."

Dan flinched at the reminder. "Maybe. But that's also the reason why nothing will ever happen between us. As long as Aida is tied to the lamp, there's too much of an imbalance between us. I don't want to ever put her into a position where she's unable to say no."

Jasper's face fell for a moment, but then just as quickly brightened again. "Well, that's easy enough. You just need to find a way to break the bindings."

A humorless laugh escaped him. "You know I've been looking into it. Unfortunately, there aren't a lot of resources available on Genie magic."

Their conversation was interrupted by the jingling of the bell above the front door.

"Well, well, well. I seem to have missed the notice that this shop was under new management."

Ice flowed through Dan's veins, and Jasper met his eyes with a look of panic. He pushed away from the chair and stepped through the door, pushing Jasper behind him. Hakim stood just inside the door, hands clasped behind his back and looking around the room with exaggerated interest. His magistrate's crest glistened in the sun falling through the small front window.

"How can I help you, Hakim?" Dan didn't bother to hide the ice in his tone.

Hakim clucked his tongue. "That's 'Your Honor,' to you, street rat."

"Did you need a pair of pants let out?" Jasper asked from behind Dan's shoulder. "You look like there's a little more of you than the last time we met."

Dan threw an elbow behind him, but it was too late. Hakim gave the boy a venomous glare, but he kept his words directed at Dan. "You seem to have misplaced your employer."

"We were dismissed."

It wasn't technically true, but Dan would argue that being left to die in the desert was a pretty clear declaration of severance.

And if he demands repayment, we have more than enough to cover the necklace now.

Hakim looked unconvinced. "Were you now? And you just happened to suddenly procure the money needed to purchase this shop so soon after leaving his service?" He stepped closer and leaned in, only stopped from invading Dan's space by the counter between them. "Careful, Aladdin. I smell a thief."

Dan kept his spine straight and his voice even. "I stole nothing. The bill of sale was filed with the appropriate authorities. The shop is mine."

"For now. But we'll see how long business lasts when your customers realize what kind of man they're dealing with. A street rat and a pickpocket? It won't take much time for your customers to realize they should take their business elsewhere."

Jasper shifted, muttering something under his breath, and Dan shot an arm out behind him to keep the boy in place. No matter how false his accusations were, Hakim was still the chief magistrate, and assaulting him was a quick path to the gallows. "Are you threatening me?"

Hakim finally leaned back, a satisfied smirk on his face. "I'm just stating facts. You might think you can find a life here, but a street rat will always be a street rat, and I'll ensure you make your way back to the gutter where you belong."

A throat cleared behind the magistrate.

"What's interesting to me is that you must have spent a great deal of time in the gutter in order to know its inhabitants so well." Aida's voice dripped with disdain.

Hakim spun on his heel, and his eyes widened. He faltered backward a step, clearly flustered at the sight before him.

Aida stood in the open doorway, arms crossed and eyes blazing. The plain brown shawl she wore over her head and shoulders to grant her some anonymity as she walked the streets had fallen, hanging low around her back and revealing her delicate, jeweled headdress and matching necklace. Her fitted top and flowing skirt were a deep ruby red the same color as her stained lips.

Hakim faltered, "You—you're—"

"Princess Aida of Jinnal," Aida answered coldly with a haughty lift of her chin.

The magistrate bowed low, his attitude suddenly all obsequious pandering. "Your Highness, how might I be of service to you today? Are you lost? In search of a dressmaker? I know of a lovely woman just down the street who would be able to assist you in whatever you need. A shop like this is no place for a lady. Perhaps you would allow me the honor of accompanying you?"

Aida stared at him for a long moment before blinking slowly twice. "My, you certainly do love to hear yourself talk. Mister—"

Hakim cleared his throat. "The correct term of address is 'Your Honor.' I'm not sure how things are done in Jinnal, but here in El-Huram the office of chief magistrate is held in high regard." He gave her a greasy smile and puffed his chest out proudly, no doubt to draw attention to the silver crest.

Aida was unimpressed. "In Jinnal, it is uncustomary for those who hold civil service offices to interrupt their royalty."

Hakim paled just a little.

"As I was saying, Mister...?" Her voice trailed off and she looked to Dan and Jasper.

"Hakim!" Jasper supplied gleefully.

Aida's nose wrinkled at the name, likely recalling the stories that Dan and Jasper had told her. "Mister Hakim, what gives you the impression that I am not exactly where I want to be?"

"HA!" Jasper cheered. Dan sent a warning glare over his shoulder, though internally he matched the boy's sentiments.

Hakim's smile faltered. "This is a tailor shop."

Aida raised an eyebrow. "And?"

"A princess such as yourself would much rather be taken to a seamstress or dressmaker who can suit your needs better."

She stalked forward a step, moving with a feline grace that reminded Dan of a tiger on the hunt. The fingers on her right hand twitched slightly and a breeze blew through the room, slamming the door shut behind her. Hakim retreated until he was cornered against the counter. "It's bold of you to assume to know what I want," she purred. "I assure you, *a princess such as myself* is quite capable of determining my own needs."

"But...but this is a tailor shop! And he's nothing but a beggar dressed in fancy clothes."

Dan's jaw tensed at Hakim's reminder, but he held his tongue.

Aida glanced his way, and for a moment he thought he saw a flash of warmth before she fixed her cold gaze back on Hakim. "It doesn't look like he's begging to me."

"Not now, but he's been caught stealing before. Believe me, you can't trust him."

She hummed thoughtfully and tapped her chin as she stepped back. "I see."

Hakim visibly relaxed and his bravado returned. "You understand now why I suggested you find another establishment. Please allow me to escort you out." His hand reached for her elbow.

Faster than a viper, Aida captured his wrist and twisted his arm around, pressing it against his back. She forced him into the counter and leaned in so that her mouth was right next to his ear. "You misunderstand me," she whispered dangerously. "What I meant was that I see that it is you who can't be trusted. Now, you will vacate the premises and leave this fine tailor and his assistant alone."

Hakim's squawk of protest turned into a whimper as she twisted his wrist further into his back.

"And if you ever try to touch me again, I will make sure that both the Sultan and Prince Kamaran are aware of your methods of justice. I'm not sure how it's done in El-Huram," she said, echoing his previous words, "but in Jinnal we don't turn a blind eye to slave traders."

With those words, she turned him around and shoved him towards the door. Hakim stumbled, then looked over his shoulder. His eyes burned with seething hatred. "You'll pay for this, Aladdin," he spat. "You might think you've won this time, but not even she will be enough to protect you forever." The door slammed shut after him, rattling the walls.

A thick tension hung in the air.

Jasper cleared his throat. "Aida, that was terrifying." He paused. "Can you teach me?"

Ten

Aida

Dinner was fast becoming Aida's least favorite time of day. It wasn't because of the food, which was delicious, or the dining room, which was a feast for the eyes with sparkling gold and crystal furnishings and polished marble. It wasn't the musicians who were hired to provide background music at every meal, or even the fact that humans seemed to have a strange fascination with the number and size of forks used at a formal dinner.

No, the reason for her dislike lay entirely in the company.

"Tell me more about the mines," Kamaran said as he placed another stuffed grape leaf—one she hadn't asked for—on Aida's plate. "It still amazes me that such a small country should have the fortune of such a rich resource."

Aida smiled tightly at him. "I don't know what else there is to say that I haven't already said, Kamaran. We simply have been blessed." When Kamaran wasn't looking, she sent the grape leaf back to the platter.

"But you already brought along such a large number of gems. Surely the mines must be nearly depleted by now."

Perhaps—if they actually existed. Humans really place value on the silliest things.

"I'm sure there are plenty more where those came from."

"Kamaran, for goodness' sake, do stop badgering the poor girl about trade," the Sultan spoke up from the end of the long table, a spoon of soup halfway to his mouth. "I'm sure she gets her fill of the subject during the day."

Aida shot him a grateful smile, and he winked in return.

Kamaran laughed easily. "You're quite right, Father. Well, Aida? What would you like to talk about instead?"

I would rather be talking with Dan about Jasper and his plans for a tiger. Or about the shop and all his projects.

She pushed the troubling thought aside.

If Kamaran and I are married, we'll be having dinner conversations like this all the time. Surely it can't be that hard.

"Why don't you tell me about your day?" she ventured.

The prince pulled a face. "My day?"

"Yes. What did you do? How did you occupy your time?"

He waved her words away. "Boring meetings, mostly—a bunch of policy and civilian issues that I won't go into detail about, lest I put you to sleep." He leaned closer and lowered his voice. "There's a party tomorrow night at the Hanging Gardens that I'm going to escape to, if you'd like to come with me."

"Won't you be missed? I would think that a meeting important enough to be held after dinner would be something you should attend."

"Eh, maybe. But it's not like anything interesting is ever discussed. It's always the same thing over and over again: how do we fix the situation in the slums? What are we doing to improve living conditions? Are crime rates going up, and what can we do to prevent that?"

Aida immediately thought of Dan and his efforts. "Aren't those things that interest you, though? You're the future Sultan, after all."

"That's what I'll have advisors for. Those stuffy old men can all sit in the room and make boring decisions. But that's enough uninteresting talk. Come with me to the party?" Kamaran picked up her hand and turned it over before pressing a kiss to her palm. "I want to be able to walk in with the most beautiful girl in El-Huram on my arm."

Aida waited for the butterflies that she knew should result from the attention. Kamaran was handsome and charming, and he was certainly treating her with an attentiveness that would suggest affection. But she found he was also shallow and lazy, and his interest tended to wax and wane depending on how he felt she could improve his social standing.

But remember the goal. As his princess, you'll never have to serve anyone ever again. You'll have freedom.

She gently pulled her hand away and gave him a bright, false smile. "Of course. I would love to."

"Princess Aida, if I might have a moment?"

Aida pulled to a surprised stop outside the dining room doors as the Sultan joined her.

"Of course, Your Majesty." She inclined her head respectfully. "My time is yours to command."

The words came automatically, and Aida realized with a rush of surprise that, for the first time in hundreds of years, they were not true.

Because my time is Dan's, and he's never asked for more of it than I'm willing to give.

The sudden revelation was so heavy that she nearly missed the Sultan's next words.

"Oh, no. My own time is burden enough; you can keep yours. But perhaps you would accompany me on a stroll in the garden?"

He held out an inviting arm while waiting for her answer, and Aida couldn't help but compare his treatment of her to the other two men who had both demanded her escort that day. As Sultan, he could absolutely demand that she walk with him, and yet he was politely and patiently waiting.

How very unlike his son.

"Of course, Your Majesty." Aida linked her arm through his and they walked out into the cool night air. The gardens in this part of the palace were much grander and carefully cultivated than the little bit of wildness out-side her room. The hedges were carefully trimmed with sharp lines and rounded edges, and there were topiary animals interspersed among the flowers at various intervals. The sand paths were straight and level, and not a stray weed could be seen within their bounds. A long water feature ran down the length of the center, with colored floating lanterns adding a touch of magic and whimsy.

The Sultan was quiet for the first few moments, content to simply walk and study the garden around them.

Then, "I thought you should know that he means to propose a marriage alliance."

The statement was so sudden that it took Aida's brain a moment to catch up. "Does he?" It was easier than she expected to keep the eagerness from her voice.

This is what I've been dreaming about for years. Shouldn't I be more excited?

"He does. Kamaran is quite taken with the idea of you and Jinnal. He has informed me that he intends to propose during the Festival next week."

Though his tone was conversational, Aida could sense that there was something amiss. "Is there a reason you're telling me this, Your Majesty? Shouldn't I be hearing it from Kamaran?"

"I'm telling you now so that you understand that you have my permission and blessing to tell him no. In fact, I encourage you to do so."

Aida tensed. "You disapprove?"

The Sultan patted the hand that held his arm. "Of you? Not at all. Only the idea of a marriage between the two of you."

"I'm afraid I'm not following."

They came upon a stone bench, and he motioned for her to sit before taking his place beside her. "You are a charming young woman, Aida. You are poised and intelligent, and I get the sense that there is much more to you than meets the eye. You come from a country whose wealth would only strengthen us, and I have no doubt that you would be able to keep my son in line."

Aida folded her hands carefully in her lap. "Those certainly sound like good things."

"And they would be...if Kamaran felt any degree of real affection at all." He sighed, and suddenly Aida saw the weight of ruling a country and managing a wayward son fall upon his shoulders. "But as it stands now, he sees you as a prize to be won and paraded around. He does not see Jinnal as a true ally, but rather a means to further his own desires and way of living. As I said, he quite likes the *idea* of you. But the real Princess Aida, the one who hides deep thoughts behind those big brown eyes and who stifles passion under pretty smiles? Her he knows nothing about. He does not see that you find his constant attention stifling at best, nor does he appreciate the way that you can insult a fawning man in such a way as to leave him thinking you paid a compliment."

Aida's eyes were wide. "You've been watching me."

"Of course, my dear. I make it a point to pay attention to all the possible candidates for marriage. To be completely honest, you would be exactly the kind of princess that Adhavi needs, but I am not so blind as to believe that Kamaran is what *you* need."

Aida was quiet for a moment, absorbing this new and surprising information. "I see. So you would like me to refuse him?"

The Sultan patted her hand, the action so kind and fatherly that it caused tears to prick at the corner of her eyes. "That's ultimately up to you, my dear. I'm simply letting you know that you have a choice. Don't let Kamaran pressure you into an answer and a life you don't really want."

With a final pat, he stood and left her in the garden with her thoughts.

But marrying Kamaran—being a princess—it is what I want. It's everything I've ever wished for.

Isn't it?

The Hanging Gardens turned out to be a large glass greenhouse that had been transformed into a party space. The floor was covered in colorful tile patterns, with a space in the middle cleared out to be a dance floor. Potted plants of every size and variety filled the edges and corners and served as a natural barrier between the dance floor and a private dining area. A miniature hedge maze took up nearly a third of the building, with cozy, sequestered nooks and splashing fountains. True to its name, planters hung from the ceiling as well at different heights, and the cascading ferns, colorful flowering vines, and wide leaves made the room feel like the middle of a rainforest.

The air was damp and warm and, had Aida not harnessed a bit of cool air to circulate around her legs and neck, she would have been dabbing sweat from her lips and nose along with the rest of the women.

Kamaran kept her close at his side, his arm never straying far from her waist as he made his way around the room. It was clear from his interactions with the other guests that he was a crowd favorite, and Aida found herself on the receiving end of a number of dirty looks from some of the other women.

They had been standing and mingling for nearly two hours when Kamaran pulled her over to greet a small group of young men who looked to be around his own age. They greeted him enthusiastically. "Prince Kam the Man!"

Aida barely contained her snort at the ridiculous nickname.

Kamaran seemed to eat it up. "Jamal. Rahim. Yusef." He shook each of their hands and gave them all a wide smile. "It's good to see you here."

The one he had greeted as Rahim, a short fellow with a pointed goatee and a half-empty glass in his hand, slowly looked Aida up and down, bold appreciation in his gaze. She shivered, suddenly feeling vulnerable and exposed, despite the fact that her emerald dress covered everything from her neck down to the top of her shoes, leaving only her arms and shoulders bare.

"And who is this gorgeous creature?"

Aida opened her mouth to correct him on the only appropriate use of the word "creature" in polite conversation, but Kamaran cut her off.

"This is Princess Aida of Jinnal." He ran his hand down her arm and picked up her hand, dropped a kiss on her fingertips before tucking it possessively into the crook of his arm. "She's been visiting Adhavi the last few weeks."

The action, Aida supposed, was meant to be romantic, but all it served to do was make her feel like a coveted accessory.

"How does one go about finding a visiting princess?" Yusef, slightly portly and with prematurely thinning hair, was just as blatant in his perusal as Rahim. He waggled his eyebrows at Kamaran. "And would you be open to sharing?"

Aida clenched her jaw and tried to pull her hand free, but Kamaran squeezed his arm close to his side, capturing her.

"Sorry, fellows," he answered with a laugh. "This one is all mine."

Yusef shrugged. "Ah, well. Can't blame a man for trying."

Actually, yes. I can and do blame you for trying.

"Does she have sisters?" Rahim waved over a server and exchanged his now empty glass for a full one.

Aida's smile turned brittle. She subtly tried tugging her arm free again.

Jamal cleared his throat. Of the three, he was closest to Kamaran in height and build, and he had a messy, careless look about him that Aida supposed made many girls swoon. "Her Highness is right here, Yusef," he scolded, smacking the other man in the back of the head.

Finally, someone with a modicum of manners.

"You should at least ask her yourself." He smirked. "Do you have any sisters?"

I take it back.

Aida finally succeeded in pulling her arm free. "It has been charming, gentlemen," she lied through her teeth. "But I find myself in need of something to drink. If you'll excuse me."

She turned on her heel, not knowing exactly where she was going other than away from Kamaran and his abhorrent friends. She strode quickly along the edge of the dance floor.

"Aida, wait!" Kamaran quickly caught up to her, slipping an arm around her waist. "Why did you leave like that? You made me look silly."

She gave him a flat look from the corner of her eye. "I told you: I'm thirsty."

"There was no need to run off." He pulled her to a stop and lifted his hand, snapping his finger at a server passing on the other side of the room. Like magic, the man immediately hastened to his side. Kamaran swiped two glasses of sparkling juice and dismissed the server without so much as a thank you. He handed her one.

"That was rude," Aida chided him, taking a sip of the sweet drink. "Why didn't you thank him?"

"Thank him?" Kamaran looked at her as if she were speaking another language. "Why would I thank him? He's just doing his job."

"But he obviously was on his way somewhere else and had to stop and run all the way over here."

"Again: it's his job, Aida. He's a server. He serves. I'm a prince. I command. You're a princess. You stand there and look ravishing."

Is this really what I thought I wanted? Aida looked out at the room, and the clear distinction between the guests and the wait staff. *To sit and demand service as if it's a right to have others do my bidding? As if they were the ones bound to a lamp?* Her stomach soured.

As if I were the master instead of the Genie?

"Oh no, we can't have that. Where's your pretty smile gone to?" Aida started as Kamaran's fingers touched her frowning lips.

She immediately pulled back. "I think I'm going to go."

His eyebrows shot to the top of his forehead. "But the night is still young; the party isn't even halfway over yet."

"I know, but I—"

"Dance with me," he commanded, tugging her to the dance floor. He took her hand and set his other against her upper back, pulling her quite close.

She pushed against his chest to reclaim some space. "Kamaran, I don't really want to dance."

He smiled suggestively. "I would be willing to explore a corner of the hedge maze instead if you wanted."

She blew out an exasperated breath. "No, I don't want that, either."

Kamaran stopped, throwing his hands up in the air and rolling his eyes. He grabbed her arm and pulled her roughly to the side, speaking in a low hiss. "We're at a party, Aida. There's dancing, there's food, there's merriment. It's fun. What else do you want?"

"To not be subjected to lewd comments, for one."

He gave her a look of disbelief as he wrapped his arms around her again, leading her through the steps but still keeping to the side. "Is that all? They didn't mean anything by it."

"Then they shouldn't have said it."

His shoulders fell. "You're right. I'll talk to them about it."

"Thank you." She nodded sharply.

"But other than that, are you having a good time?" He wore such a hopeful, vulnerable expression that Aida found some of her frustration melting away. It was moments like these when she saw signs of what kind of man he could be, if only he would stop focusing on himself.

"It's a lovely place," she answered, looking up at the plants above. "Definitely unique, and the flowers are truly gorgeous."

"Not as gorgeous as you." The prince was looking at her with his charming smile again. He leaned closer to whisper in her ear, "To be honest, I've been dying to ask you to dance all night because it meant I would have an excuse to hold you in my arms."

His head moved away, and Aida realized with a blazing panic that he was about to kiss her. She threw her hand up in front of her mouth, stopping him.

"I'm sorry. I need to go." She pushed him away.

"Aida, wait. You can't just leave by yourself. The streets are dangerous at night for a woman alone."

She was already walking. "I'll be fine. Oh, and Kamaran?" She looked over her shoulder to find him standing dazed and confused just a few feet behind her, a hand stretched out as if to invite her back.

"Find better friends."

Eleven

Aida

She walked without really considering her direction, and somehow Aida's steps took her to Bayid street and to Dan's front door. It was well past sundown, the time he normally closed the shop, and as Aida had already been there earlier in the day to fulfill her lamp-proximity-quota, there was no reason for her to believe that Dan was still in. It was more than likely that he had retired to his upstairs apartment hours ago.

She hesitated outside the door. *I could just go back to the palace. There's no need for me to be here.*

But she had already dismissed Samira for the night, unwilling to make the poor girl stay up late when Aida could easily see to herself, and the idea of sitting in her room alone was too much. She craved company, even if it was just the shadow of Dan's presence in his shop.

With that thought, she opened the lock and silenced the bell with a snap, then carefully closed and locked the door behind her. She was surprised to find the dim glow of candlelight in the workroom when she turned around.

Is he still here? I thought for sure the shop would be empty.

A rush of unexpected happiness filled her at the thought, and she wound her way silently behind the counter and to the workroom door. Dan sat at his table, hunched over a bundle of deep purple fabric. His needle moved up and down rapidly, and he hummed a catchy melody in a minor key as he worked. The flickering flame cast shadows on his face, highlighting the planes of his cheeks, and Aida was reminded of the first time they had met. She had thought him objectively handsome then, but now she knew that the masculine beauty of his face was outshone by the beauty of his heart.

She quickly shoved the thoughts away as soon as they surfaced.

It's only because I was just with Kamaran and his friends. It doesn't take much to be better than them.

As if feeling her eyes on him, Dan suddenly looked up. "Aida!" He scrambled to his feet, bundling the fabric and shoving it behind him like a child caught with a honey cake before dinner. "What are you doing here? How long have you been standing there?"

"Only since the last chorus of your song." Aida twisted her hands together, suddenly unsure of her decision to stay. "Am I bothering you?"

Dan stepped over the various piles on the floor to join her on the other side of the workbench. "Not at all; I simply wasn't expecting you. Is everything all right? I thought you were going to a party with the prince tonight." A muscle twitched under his eyes as he said the words, but his expression remained one of concern.

"I'm fine. The party just proved to be...underwhelming, so I left."

He studied her for a long moment, as if testing the veracity of her words. "Alright. Are you hungry? Jasper made some stew and flatbread for dinner. It's cold now, but I could heat it up for you."

In truth, she was starving, but Aida shook her head. "I'm fine."

I can just magic something to eat later.

"Hmmm. Well, you've reminded me that I'm hungry, so I think I'll go bring some down. It'll just be a few minutes; make yourself at home."

Dan disappeared through a side door in the main room that led up a narrow set of stairs to the apartment above. Aida allowed herself a fond smile. She knew what Dan was doing—he was pretending to be hungry himself in order to give him an excuse to bring the food down for her.

He's taking care of me without being asked.

Just like the way he looked after his fellow citizens of El-Huram, giving his time and effort to ensure that their lives were a little better, or the way he worked tirelessly to give Jasper a good home.

To be sure, he could be more than a little over-protective, and he did have a tendency to jump right into doing what he thought was best for others, rather than asking what they wanted, but she appreciated the heart behind it. He cared—truly cared—about the people around him.

Aida hugged herself as she wandered aimlessly through the workroom. Her eyes landed on the lamp, still carefully tucked away in a little corner of the shelves. She picked it up and turned it over in her hands.

Not once in the last three weeks did Dan give any indication of using his wishes. In fact, he seemed to go out of his way to forget that he had any authority over her at all.

"Why couldn't Dan have been the prince?" she whispered into the stillness of the room before returning the lamp to its place.

The bundle of purple fabric, hastily shoved into the back of the chair, caught her eye. Curious, Aida beckoned the fabric with her fingers, causing it to fly from the chair into her waiting hands. It was the softest silk she had ever touched, buttery smooth and cold against her skin. She held it up and let the ends fall towards the floor in a cascade of purple.

It was a dress.

The sleeves were long and loose, with a high neckline in front and cut low and draping in the back. The floor-length skirt had a short train that pooled around Aida's feet.

"It was supposed to be a surprise." Dan released a doleful sigh from outside the door of the workroom. "Though I suppose it will be easier to do the fittings now that you know." He set a tray holding two bowls of steaming stew and a pile of flatbread on the counter behind him before approaching.

Tears gathered in the corners of Aida's eyes. "You're making me a dress?"

Dan shrugged and sheepishly rubbed the back of his neck. "I saw the fabric and it made me think of you."

"But you're a tailor. You hem and mend and make repairs. This is—this is different." The lump at the back of her throat made speaking hard.

He winced. "I know. It's been a long time since I made a garment from scratch. It might be horrible, but—"

"Why?" Aida interrupted, suddenly desperate to know the answer.

"Why what?"

"Why are you going to all the trouble to make me a dress? This is more than just extending your normal work day, Dan. This is time and effort that you could be spending doing something else. Why are you making me a dress when you know I can just make whatever I want by myself?"

A soft, warm light filled Dan's eyes and he held her gaze as he stepped forward, closing the distance between them. He wrapped his hands around hers, still holding the half-finished dress. "I'm making you a dress because even though you could do it yourself, I want you to know that you don't have to. I want you to know that you are worth any amount of time and effort. I want you to know that you could spend the rest of your life not doing a lick of magic, and you would still be taken care of." He broke eye contact to look down at the purple silk between them. "Every time you wear this dress, I want you to know you're not alone."

The earnestness of his tone, the depth of emotion in his eyes, and the warm pressure of his hands on her own were the final blow to the floodgates of her emotions. After centuries of loneliness and abuse, the idea that someone could care about her so selflessly was too much for her heart to handle. With a strangled sob, she hugged the dress to her chest and fell forward into Dan's arms.

He held her for what felt like hours as she cried, rubbing gentle circles on her back and stroking her hair. Finally, when the last tears had been spent, Aida took a deep, shuddering breath and stepped back. She swiped a hand at her gritty, swollen eyes. "I'm sorry."

Dan shoved his hands into his pockets and gave her a gentle smile. "You don't have to apologize for having emotions, Aida. It's only human."

She hugged her arms around her middle. The room felt much colder now that she was outside the warm circle of Dan's arms. "But I'm not human. I'm a Genie."

"You're right," he teased. "That means your tears are probably magical, aren't they? It means my shirt will never fade or wear out."

Aida winced as she saw the dark, wet circle she had left above his heart. "No, but I can fix—"

"Aida," he interrupted, gently touching her elbow, "I was only teasing. I don't mind. I'm honored that you felt safe enough to share your emotions with me."

She thought she had run out of tears, but more threatened to spill. She gave him a watery smile.

"Now, I don't know about you, but I'm still a little hungry." Dan stepped around her, his hand slipping from her elbow and skating along her waist in the softest of touches, sending shivers up her spine. He stepped out of the room long enough to pick up the tray, then gestured with his head to the workroom floor. "Shall we?"

She trailed behind him as he spread out some of the used garments on the floor, creating a sort of picnic blanket. "I know it's not the royal dining room you're used to." He sank cross-legged to the ground and patted the space next to him. "But a picnic every once in a while is good for the soul."

"Oh really?" She accepted the bowl of stew he handed her, sending a tiny frisson of magic through her fingers to warm the contents. The smell of savory meat and rich spices rose to meet her nose, and her mouth watered in response. "Where did you hear that?"

"Jasper," he answered with a grin before shoving a spoon into his mouth. "He went through a phase a few years ago where he refused to eat at a normal table. Apparently, his friend Malik and his sisters were at a party with a picnic, and it was all they could talk about for weeks. It's amazing the things that little kids will latch onto."

Aida smiled, well able to imagine the exuberance with which Jasper would have embraced the idea. "You've been together for quite a while, haven't you?"

Dan nodded. "Almost seven years now. He was six years old when he tried to pick my pocket the first time and failed. My father was a tailor, and he had sewn false pockets in my trousers. Jasper was so upset that he started crying and throwing a tantrum. The man in charge of the orphanage where he was staying was running a little side business, teaching the children how to pickpocket and then sending them out to 'work' for their supper. Jasper knew that if he didn't come home with enough, he would be sent to bed with a beating instead of dinner."

Aida's hands curled into fists. "That's awful."

Humans really have no limit to the depths of depravity they will sink to.

"It was. I felt bad, so I offered him what little I had in my real pockets—I was just a beggar at the time myself, so it wasn't much. He came back the following day, and the one after that, and the one after that until finally I decided that it would be easiest if he just came with me."

"You must have been young at the time." Aida studied him. "You can't be more than a few decades old."

"I was sixteen. I'd already been on the streets for a number of years at that point." Dan looked around the room. "It's still kind of surreal to be back in this place."

A comfortable silence filled the space between them. Dan held out his hand for her empty bowl, stacking it with his own. The sight made a sudden guilty thought fly into her head, and she gasped.

"What's wrong?" His eyes were sharp with concern.

"Your food. It was cold." Here he was, doing everything in his power to make sure that she was taken care of, and she didn't think of anyone beyond herself.

He relaxed. "It's fine. Yours was, too."

"But it wasn't. I warmed it up using magic, and I should have thought to do the same for you, but I didn't, and—"

"Aida," he interrupted, grabbing one of her hands to get her attention. "It's fine. I'm a man; I will eat practically anything as long as it's not rotting. Cold stew is nothing."

"But it was only cold because I was crying for so long." Her brows pulled together into a frown. "Why didn't you ask me to fix it?"

"Because it wasn't your responsibility. If I wanted it warm, I could have done it myself." He squeezed her fingers. "You don't have to do anything for me."

She looked down at his hands, calloused and warm against her skin. Several times that night he had reached for her hands or arms, but it was so different from the way Kamaran touched her. The prince's touch didn't cause her stomach to dance with a swarm of butterflies, and it certainly didn't make her feel safe and cared for.

He's your master, not your friend.

But Aida desperately wished he could be.

A tension was building in the air, thickening the longer she stayed silent. Panic seized her, and she grasped for the first question that came to her mind.

"Why does Hakim hate you?"

Like the sun clearing away the mist after a rain, the strange tension dissipated. Dan chuckled. "That's an unexpected question." He released her hands and stretched out his legs, leaning back onto his elbows.

"But important. I should know what kind of criminals I'm consorting with."

He gave her an amused look. "I feel like I should be offended that you've already decided our guilt."

"You already said yourself that Jasper was a pickpocket," she pointed out.

"Fair enough. Though, in the case of Hakim, it has less to do with anything that I've done and more to do with what my father did."

"What does that mean?"

"Though my father came from a family of tailors, my mother was the daughter of one of the Sultan's advisors. Father did some work for him, which is how they met. Needless to say, her family was less than pleased when she announced her intention to marry a lowly tailor."

Aida mirrored his posture. "Having witnessed what I have of humanity, I can't say I'm surprised. But what does this have to do with Hakim?"

"He was the boy my mother was supposed to marry, had she gone along with her family's expectations."

"Oh."

Dan gave her a grim smile. "Yes. He never forgave my father for stealing away the future he had envisioned for himself—never mind the fact that Mother would never have married him anyway. After they died, he was the one who fought to have the shop sold, claiming that my father's unfulfilled contracts were akin to debts, and they needed to be paid."

"That's absurd. No one in their right mind would accept that for a second."

"Except he was already a magistrate, and the chief magistrate at the time was a friend of his family." Dan sighed. "It's all a matter of who you know."

The injustice of it all burned in her chest. "But what about your grandparents? Surely they had something to say about their grandson being forced into the streets."

"They disowned Mother when she got married. I tried contacting them once, right after she died, but my grandfather said that as far as he was concerned, he never had a daughter, and he certainly didn't have a grandson."

Aida could hear the hurt in his voice, and it struck a chord deep within her, stirring up feelings she long ago wanted to forget.

"Sometimes the people who are supposed to love you the most are the ones who hurt you the worst."

Dan shifted, turning to his side and propping his head on his hand. He regarded her curiously. "Spoken like someone with firsthand experience."

There was an unspoken invitation in his words. Aida knew him well enough by now to know that he would never force the words from her, but was she really ready to open the door on all those emotions again? She had already cried more that night than she had in decades. Besides, the story was one that had never been told to another soul. It was a secret she guarded close, afraid of what would happen if she allowed herself to be vulnerable again.

Dan watched her, silent and waiting, and it was his steady patience that won out in the end.

She took a deep breath.

"I had an uncle..."

Twelve

Aida

Before...

Aida skipped along the narrow path, watching in fascination as each stone ahead materialized from nothing. Rainbows of light swirled on either side, coalescing into window-like portals when she looked at them directly. Mountain ranges, verdant jungles, endless plains, lush forests—all of them only a step off the path and a thought away. She had listened with envious attentiveness to all her cousins' stories of traveling by Genie Ways, but she had never been old enough to experience it herself.

Until now.

"Where are we going, Merroc?"

Her uncle looked over his shoulder and smiled at her indulgently. "The same place I said we were going the last time you asked. I have a business partner to meet near the Agrabian Sea, and then from there we'll be heading to Badroul."

Aida's heart gave a leap of excitement at the mention of the capital city. "What are we going to be doing in Badroul?"

"Hmmm," Merroc turned his face back towards the path ahead as he hummed mysteriously. Though he was her uncle, the years separating him from her father were many, and at two hundred years old, he was hardly much older than herself, who was just on the cusp of adulthood. His face was young and handsome, and Aida had seen him garnering more than his fair share of female attention. He tapped a finger thoughtfully against his chin. "I think perhaps we should pay a visit to the Registry."

Aida squealed and jumped forward, throwing her hands around his neck and nearly forcing them both off the path and through a portal to an icy tundra. "You mean it's really happening?"

Merroc laughed and untangled her arms from his neck, setting her gently back on the path. "It's really happening," he confirmed. "Your father gave me instructions just this morning. I only have to take care of this bit of business first."

She squealed again, clasping her hands together in front of her chest while her feet excitedly tapped against the magical stones beneath her. "I can't believe it's really happening!" She suddenly paused. "But it's so soon. Does Father really think I'm ready?"

Merroc covered her hands with his own, giving her the same confident smile she had known all her life. "Aida, you're one of the most powerful Genies we've seen in three generations. You have more magic in one finger than some of our cousins have in their whole bodies. You'll pass the test just fine; this whole trip is a testament to that fact."

Bright curiosity burned through the warmth of his praise. "What do you mean?"

Merroc gestured to the swirling lights around them. "You've never traveled by Genie Ways before, so you wouldn't know. Aida, when the rest of us travel, we see *one* destination—the portal ahead. Everything on either side is just darkness."

Aida cocked her head to the side as she surveyed the portals. "This isn't normal?"

A short laugh escaped him. "No. Even your father, with his Royal Magic, can't make more than two or three portals appear at a time. He doesn't have them simply waiting for a mere glance to form them into existence."

Aida, now more eager than ever to continue their journey, started walking again. "But what about you? You have just as much magic as Father—I've heard him say so myself."

"But still not as much as you, little niece. You are a true treasure."

Aida leaned against the weathered wood of the small fishing hut. She wasn't sure what kind of business her uncle had inside such a rundown and dilapidated building, but he seemed to regard it as quite important, judging by the way he got more and more nervous as they approached. His business partner had looked even more off-putting than the building, with a hood he had worn down low over his face and dark, beady eyes that had watched her with unsettling intensity.

His mouth had stretched into a wide, wolfish smile at the sight of her, and it was all she could do to keep her own smile of greeting in place.

"Wait here for me, Aida," Merroc had said before following the fellow inside. She had been only too happy to comply.

That had been nearly a half hour before, and Aida amused herself by flicking a flower in and out of existence, experimenting with the color and number of petals each time. Her magic was as natural as breathing. She could feel it, like a well of deep water in the very center of her being, and she simply drew it up and fashioned it into whatever idea took hold of her fancy. How much more would she be able to do once she was registered and could train and study more seriously? Her future was wide open and limitless.

"Aida."

Merroc's voice was strangely distant and hollow as he called her name. She scrambled to her feet. "Yes, Mer?"

"I need you to come inside for a moment."

Aida's eyes widened in surprise, but she did as he directed, squeezing the flower into nothing as her hands fell to her sides. She slipped past Merroc's stiff form through the open doorway and immediately halted.

From the outside, the structure appeared to be a simple fisherman's shed, but as Aida crossed the threshold, she realized that the weathered wood and boarded windows were simply a facade to hide the fact that it was a Genie realm—a pocket of space larger on the inside than the outside that could be accessed only by those with permission from the owner.

Merroc placed a hand on the small of her back and urged her forward. "Come in, Aida. There's someone here I would like you to meet."

Aida turned to him with wide eyes. "Is this his realm?"

Merroc laughed mirthlessly. "No, it's mine."

"But I thought—"

"No questions right now, Aida." His sharp words cut her off.

Sandstone walls lit by glowing torches gave the room an almost cave-like feel. For the moment, a tall pedestal stood in the center, though Aida knew that could change depending on Merroc's needs. In the center of the pedestal stood a golden oil lamp, with a delicate spout for the wick and a perfectly rounded handle. Red and purple gems dotted the flared base, and as Aida drew closer, she could see the intricate filigree etchings that decorated the surface.

"So, this is her." Merroc's business partner stepped forward and threw his hood back, revealing dark, oiled hair and gold-hooped ears. His eyes ran up and down the length of her, and he nodded. "I think she'll do quite nicely."

Aida took a step back, colliding with Merroc's chest. His hands grasped her upper arms. "Do nicely for what, Mer? What's going on?"

Merroc stepped around her and plucked up the lamp. He stood for a moment with his back to her, studying it, and when he turned around again, his face was completely transformed. Gone was her handsome, genial uncle, the one who had spent countless hours with her in the library, pouring over maps and dreaming of travels to other lands and realms, who had been at her side when her magic had first appeared, who had guided her through all her training. In his place was a cold, dark stranger. He wore Merroc's face, but the eyes were all wrong.

He handed her the lamp, and in her surprise and shock, Aida took it without thinking. As soon as her fingers closed around it, she felt the change.

Invisible shackles burned into her wrists and ankles, and a heavy weight settled over her shoulders, pressing her down to her knees, along with the sensation of a rope tying itself around her chest and pulling tight. Aida cried out in pain and surprise.

"Merroc, what are you doing?"

Her uncle looked down at her. A brief flash of something like regret passed in his eyes, before being replaced by cold calculation.

"Tell me, Aida. What do you know about humans?"

"They're weak and powerless. They have no magic, and they die easily." Aida blinked against the tears that stung the corners of her eyes.

"They also pay handsomely for something that will give them even a taste of having magic. Imagine the kind of reward they would part with for the magic of the most powerful Genie in three generations? We're not all like you, little niece. We can't just make unlimited riches appear."

Aida's eyes widened with fear. Her mouth tried and failed to find words to answer.

"It's nothing personal, Aida. This is purely a business decision. Now, go into your little lamp and wait while I speak with your new master."

Despite her efforts to fight it, in the space of a breath Aida was no longer in the sandstone room, but was instead standing on something hard and cold, completely surrounded by darkness. She snapped her fingers, calling a flame to life.

Shiny metal enclosed her on all sides, curving up and away from the floor into a rounded dome above her head. Aida ran to the closest wall and pounded against it with her fists. "Let me out! Merroc!"

Voices, muffled as if from a distance, drifted down to her ears.

"It's done then?" Merroc's partner asked.

"It's done. She is bound to the lamp now, and any wish made by the owner of the lamp she is obligated to fulfill." Merroc spoke as calmly as if he were speaking of the weather.

"*Any* wish?" The greed was so evident in the man's voice that Aida could picture him rubbing his hands together as he said the words.

"Any that does not fall under her natural limitations. But have no fear—I have been training with Aida for years now, and not even I have found a limit to what she can do. Now, the payment?"

She pounded against the walls and screamed until her hands were bruised and her throat was raw. With a final, defeated sob, Aida slid down the cold metal and sank to the ground. Her chest felt as if it had been ripped open, but the shock of betrayal left her mind numb. Her hands fell limply to her sides as she stared into darkness.

A tiny pinprick of light from above was the only con-firmation she had that the outside world still existed. Having seen the lamp from the outside, she assumed that it was the end of the spout that was meant to hold the wick as it burned.

I wonder if I could get out that way?

The walls were slick, but the low ceilings meant that she might be able to jump high enough to reach the inside of the hole. With hope ignited, Aida crossed the small space and reached a hand to where the wall opened up to the spout, only to come into contact with a surface that was cold and hard as glass.

"No. No, no, no!" Aida pounded against the invisible barrier. "MERROC! Let me out!"

Immediately, she felt a strange pulling sensation that began at her feet and continued up her spine until she could feel it in the very roots of her hair. One moment she was in the lamp, and the next she was standing in a gaudily furnished room, blinking in the light of a crackling fire.

"Merroc, what did—" She stopped mid-sentence as her exhausted brain finally realized that it was not her uncle who stood before her. Merroc's beady-eyed partner held the lamp in both hands and looked her over with a greedy, delighted smile.

"What are you doing here? Where's Merroc?" Aida crossed her arms and glared at him.

"Hello, little Genie," the man answered, completely disregarding her question. "I am your master now."

She shook her head slowly, refusing to believe the words. "Where's my uncle?"

"He's not here, and none of your concern." The man set the lamp down on a gold-leafed table beside him and stalked towards her. "What you should be concerned about is how you're going to serve me."

Aida scoffed. "I'm not going to do anything for you. In fact, I was just leaving."

She turned on her heel, looking about for a door, when her elbow was seized in an iron grip.

"You will do nothing of the sort. You are mine now."

"I'm *not*! Let go of me." She yanked her arm free.

"I wish you wouldn't go."

A warm, sticky feeling slowly washed over her. Aida took a step back in the direction of the door, then gasped at the painful sensation of a vise squeezing her heart. An unseen force pulled her away from the door, and she fell forward onto her hands and knees, struggling to breathe through the pain.

"As I was saying, little Genie: I am your master now. You will do as I wish, or there will be consequences."

Aida ground her teeth together in pain and rage.

Merroc, what did you do?

"Don't worry, though. I foresee a long and prosperous relationship between the two of us. But first, let's see if you really are as useful as your uncle claims. I wish for a bag of gold."

The warm, sticky sensation returned, and, with it, a compulsion to fulfill the man's request. She stood slowly, the last bits of hope stamped out of her chest as the words were pulled from her mouth.

"Your wish is my command."

Thirteen

Dan

Dan could barely contain the rage that simmered under his skin as Aida's tale unfolded. While his own abandonment by his grandparents had stung, it was nothing compared to the betrayal that Aida must have felt. By her account, she and her uncle had been close, and for him to look her in the eye and sell her to the highest bidder...

Dan was not normally a violent person, but in that moment, he had never desired more to lay his hands on another man.

His hands were curled into tight fists, and his jaw was tense with anger. Aida exhaled a shaky breath, and her words were bitter. "So there you have it—the story of how a naive girl learned what a mistake it is to blindly trust." She twisted her bracelets. "We have a saying back home that the burned hand teaches best, but I think scars are just as effective."

She sat up and held her arms out in front of her, pushing the metal aside to reveal thick, white scars that circled around each wrist like manacles. Dan's heart broke at the sight, both because of the physical pain the injuries must have caused, and also at the constant reminder that Aida carried of the cruelty of those who were supposed to care for her. He reached out, tracing the raised skin with his thumb. His voice cracked. "Aida..."

She pulled away and shoved the bracelets back into place. "I didn't tell you so that you would feel sorry for me. I don't need your pity, Dan. You don't need to be the hero here."

He swung into a seated position, crossing his legs and leaning his elbows on his knees. He watched her closely for a moment, taking in the tension of her shoulders and the stiff set of her jaw. Behind the expressionless mask of indifference she wore like armor, her eyes swirled with pain and grief, but she kept her chin high.

"I don't pity you," he answered quietly.

Aida narrowed her eyes. "You said that once before. Do you think that I deserved this, then? That it was some sort of punishment I deserved? That there was a reason that Abba turned his back and allowed all this to happen?"

"I don't pity you, Aida; I'm angry. I hate that this happened, and I utterly detest the man who put you into this position. I'm appalled and ashamed of every human who has since found your lamp and treated you as a possession instead of a person. I'm amazed by your resilience and strength, and I'm humbled by the compassion you show to a world that has never treated you well. I don't pity you, because you're not some poor, pitiable creature. You're the strongest, most incredible person I've ever met."

Aida's eyes had dropped to her hands, which twisted together during his speech. "But why?" The words were a barely audible whisper. "Why me?"

With a silent plea for wisdom, Dan scooted close and offered his hands, palms up. Aida gave him her fingers, and he rubbed the back of her hands with his thumbs.

"If I had the answer to that question, I wouldn't need to run this shop. Sometimes the answer is simply that Abba is Abba, and I am not. But I do know that He cares for His children, and that His hands are always at work, even in the ugliest messes we make." The words settled into his own heart as he said them, as if meant for him as well as for her.

"So you're saying that He meant for this to happen." Aida used her shoulder to wipe a line of tears from her cheek. "Somehow an Abba who willingly subjects His children to pain is worse than one who doesn't care at all."

Dan was quiet for a moment, considering her words. "When Jasper was eight, he decided that he wanted to learn to cook meals for us. I warned him that he wasn't allowed to start a fire without me around to supervise, but one day he decided that he knew enough about it and was going to do it anyway. He burned himself, our tent, and almost took out our neighbors as well.

"It's obviously not exactly the same—the only thing Jas suffered was a burnt thumb, and he brought that on himself. But even though I love him and he's the only family I have, sometimes he makes choices that aren't good for him or others. I can't keep him from making those choices, but I did help him repair the damage." Dan sighed. "Sometimes awful things happen. The world is full of twisted and broken people. It's not a satisfying answer, but we just have to trust that Abba knows more about our situation than we do in the moment. He will always take care of His children, even if it's not the way we would want or expect."

Aida silently nodded, her eyes distant and unfocused. Though he wanted to say more, Dan could tell that she had reached her limit. He rose and offered her a hand up. "It's late. I should walk you back."

She wrapped her arms around her middle, looking smaller and more unsure than he had ever seen her. He wanted nothing more than to pull her into a hug again, to be the wall that stood between her and the cruelty and injustice of the outside world.

But she was in an emotional and vulnerable state at the moment, and still set on marrying the prince, so Dan shoved his hands in his pockets instead.

"I could just stay here."

He blinked and gave his head a small shake. "You what?"

She looked from him to the door and back again. "I don't want to go back and be alone in that big room right now."

Dan rubbed the back of his neck, unsure what to do.

Stay with me! his heart screamed. *Forget the prince and just stay here forever.*

His mind argued back, *She doesn't mean it like that. She's just lonely and upset right now. She's made her choice, and even if she doesn't want to be alone, having her stay here won't do her reputation any favors.*

"I—we don't—I mean..." he stumbled over his words. "We don't have a spare room."

The corners of her lips curled in amusement. "I already have a room here, silly."

"You...you do?"

Rather than answering, she grabbed his hand. After a sensation that felt rather like being poured out through a sieve and then put back together again, Dan blinked to find himself in a small, circular room. Even at its highest point, the convex ceiling was low enough that he could reach it with the tips of his fingers, and he guessed it was no more than twelve feet in diameter. The walls and ceilings were covered in brightly patterned silks draped to give the illusion of a tent. The floor was covered in soft cushions of various sizes, and a narrow daybed was shoved up against one of the curved walls and piled high with blankets. A small vanity with a circular mirror was the only other furniture in the room.

"See?" Aida gestured around them. "My room has been here the whole time."

Dan turned in a slow circle, taking in every detail. "Where are we?"

"The lamp."

"But...how? I can carry the lamp. This is definitely much bigger than that."

"It's a Genie realm—a miniature one, anyway. It's bigger on the inside."

"Not so big," he murmured. After Dan recovered from his initial surprise, he couldn't help but notice how small and cramped the room was.

She shrugged. "You get used to it after a while."

Aida had danced around the subject several times, had hinted at long stretches of time spent alone and years in between masters, but Dan saw an opportunity to get a solid answer. "How long is a while?"

"974 years, six months, and seventeen days."

Her answer was so immediate that Dan knew she must have been keeping count. His jaw dropped, but before he could follow up, she pressed ahead.

"Before you ask, yes, Genies normally do have a much longer lifespan than humans. And it wasn't all bad, I was able to make this mirror." She waved toward the vanity, and the mirror came to life, displaying the image of a fancy party in a room full of greenery and flowers. The people in the image moved, and Dan stepped closer, fascinated.

"What is this?"

"I can use it to see any part of the world that I want." Aida moved to stand by his shoulder, and they watched the mirror together. "Right now it's showing Kamaran's party, but I could also make it show this." The starry night above the desert dunes was dark and velvety. "Or this." The quiet streets of El-Huram glowed under the streetlamps. "Or this." The empty interior of Dan's shop was as familiar as his own face in the reflection.

The pieces fell into place. "This is what you meant when you said you had been watching Prince Kamaran."

Another flick of her fingers, and the mirror was plain glass again. "Yes, though that wasn't my initial intention." She hesitated. "Before Mer— before everything, I had never been able to travel Genie Ways by myself. I was so excited to be registered, because it meant that I could finally travel to all the places that I'd read of in books or heard in stories. That didn't happen, obviously. The mirror was an attempt to still be able to do that."

Aida shrugged as if it were a minor inconvenience, or an inconsequential plan that had to be abandoned. But Dan could see the longing in her eyes and hear the edge of wistfulness in her voice, and his frustration at her situation came boiling again to the surface. This was yet another part of her life that was stolen from her.

The frustration melted into determination. Dan cleared his throat and turned towards her.

She looked up at him with a question in her eyes.

He took her hand. "Aida, I wish that you could still see the world—that you could travel anywhere you wanted."

Her eyes widened, and he could see the moment that realization dawned. She threw her arms around his neck, and after a split second of hesitation, he returned the embrace. She fit perfectly in his arms, warm and soft and yet hiding a strength he could never truly fathom.

She pulled back, a dazzling smile lighting up her face and an excited sparkle in her brown eyes.

One hand waved in front of them, opening a sparkling portal, and the other grabbed hold of his hand. She tugged him forward. "Your wish is my command. What are we waiting for? I can show you the world. Let's go!"

The next few hours were a blur, as Aida pulled him from gate to gate along the Genie Way. She showed him the emerald green buildings, tall towers, and spires of Baileglas, swirled with white and flecked with black and gold. They passed through the snowy, wooded forests of Norland and the kingdom of Winterlocke, mesmerized by its cold, icy beauty. They admired the waterfalls of Azurluna, which shone like diamonds in the sunlight, and marveled at the stained glass cathedral in Streinauer and the granite columns and marble halls of D'argent. Dan's favorite was the underwater paradise of Finfolka-heem, with its colorful reef and pink coral castle. Aida's magic surrounded them in a bubble of air, allowing them to take in the myriad of sea creatures and experience the schools of glowing jellyfish in all their natural beauty.

"I never thought that I would actually be able to see any of this." Aida reclined on a beach of black sand in Twilight Kingdom, looking out at the waves that rolled in, filling the air with their soothing sound. The moonlight sparkled on the rippling surface of the water, and though Dan could feel a storm gathering in the air, the night was peaceful.

He dug into the sand and lifted a handful, letting it slowly run through the spaces between his fingers. "I hope you weren't disappointed."

"Never! It's more beautiful than I ever imagined."

Dan was mesmerized by the sight of her profile in the moonlight, by the satisfied half-smile that rested on her lips, and the tendrils of hair that shifted across her cheeks in the sea breeze.

"It is," he agreed softly, never taking his eyes from her face.

She turned and he looked away, afraid to be caught staring. "Dan!"

"What's wrong?"

"That was your second wish! You only have one left. You wasted your wish on me."

He couldn't help himself against the distress in her voice, and he threw an arm around her shoulders and scooted close enough for their legs to touch. "It wasn't wasted." He recalled the wonder and joy that lit up her face, the bright, eager curiosity in her eyes as she experienced each new place. In those moments, he could see a glimpse of the vibrant, lively, inquisitive girl she must have been. "It was worth every second."

Aida shifted toward him, leaning her head on his shoulder. His breath caught.

"Thank you," she whispered.

"Aida, I—"

His words were cut off as the ground beneath them began to shake. Dan leaped to his feet. "What's going on?"

"It's an earthquake! We should go."

Aida had the portal open in a matter of seconds, and she pulled them both through just as the shaking intensified.

She giggled. "That was close. I guess I can cross experiencing an earthquake off my list now, right underneath 'See the World.'"

Dan chuckled obligingly, but his mind was far away, still stuck in the moment on the beach. With one simple touch, a new truth had become abundantly clear:

Aida might have shown him the world, but she had somehow become everything in his.

Fourteen

Dan

Dan wasn't entirely certain how he had been invited to the Festival at the palace, but he was absolutely sure he didn't really belong. He tugged at the collar of his shirt, which seemed too tight against his throat even though he had done the sizing himself and knew it was right. The magnificent room was lit with a combination of lamps on tall lampstands standing at regular intervals along the wall, and hanging lamps that dripped with crystal beads, sending the light scattering over the floor in a dance of rainbows. A group of professional musicians gathered to one side, tuning their instruments while the rest of the guests mingled about. The room was buzzing with polite chatter and fake laughs, and everywhere that Dan looked, wealth and prestige were on display.

His eyes searched the room, never resting in one place until—there. He located the deep purple of Aida's dress. It was even more breathtaking on her than he expected, even though he had been the one to design it in the first place. Even during her last fitting, though she looked lovely, it was different seeing her completely put together under the soft glow of the ballroom lights. Her hair was pulled back in a simple braid adorned at the end with a gold band, and she wore no jewelry but her customary bangles that covered her scars. She was all fresh-faced beauty in a sea of paint and peacock-level fashion, and Dan didn't want to look away.

Until he saw whose arm she was holding, and a sick feeling rolled in the pit of his stomach.

Prince Kamaran smiled and charmed his way around the room, parading Aida about like she was his hard-won prize. He introduced her, then talked over her, and frequently waved away any words that she had to say. Aida smiled politely, but it didn't reach her eyes.

The longer Dan watched, the tighter his fists became.

"You should ask her to dance."

The voice beside him startled Dan out of his single-minded focus. He nearly yelped when he realized the Sultan was standing at his shoulder.

"I—I beg your pardon, Your Majesty." He bowed low.

The Sultan brushed the words away with a benevolent smile. "I should be the one apologizing for scaring you. But my point is still the same: you should ask her to dance."

Dan looked at him warily. He breathed slowly, trying to hide the fact that he was attempting to calm his racing heart. "Why?"

"Because I have a feeling she would enjoy it much more than she's enjoying herself now." The Sultan lifted the glass in his hand, using it to gesture to the couple.

"But that would mean taking her away from Prince Kamaran."

"And the sooner, the better, I say." He took a sip of his drink, made a face, and poured the rest into the base of a nearby potted plant. "I've never been fond of that particular juice, but Kamaran insists on having it at every social function."

Dan's mind was still endeavoring to catch up. "I don't understand...do you not approve of Princess Aida?"

"Oh, no, I approve of her. What I don't approve of is the way my son treats her, and the way he will doubtless continue to treat her if he proposes tonight like he's planning."

Dan felt the blood draining from his face. "He's planning to propose?"

"Yes, which is precisely why I advise you to go ask her to dance now. Give her something else to wish for."

"I still don't understand."

The Sultan sighed and clasped his hands behind his back. "One of the greatest fears as a parent comes from knowing that, despite all the love and training and discipline you give them, children still have the ability to make their own choices." He paused for a moment, watching as Kamaran led Aida towards another small group of over-ly-eager guests. "And sometimes those choices go against everything you've ever taught them."

At that moment, Aida's head turned in their direction, and she caught Dan's eyes from across the room.

He couldn't help the smile that overtook his face, and she turned away, blushing.

The Sultan cleared his throat. "As I said, ask her to dance. Make her see that a future full of love in a tailor shop is better than an empty one on a throne."

"But I don't—" Dan spun around, a denial of affection on his lips, only to find that the Sultan was already several steps away, weaving his way through the crowd.

Dan hesitated for just a moment before squaring his shoulders.

After all, who am I to ignore advice from my Sultan?

He crossed the room with purposeful strides and gently touched Aida's elbow. She looked over her shoulder with mingled surprise and relief. Kamaran glared daggers at him.

"Excuse me, Your Highness, but would you honor me with a dance?"

Despite the prince's protests, Aida eagerly agreed and followed Dan to the center of the room.

"Thank you," she whispered fervently. "I wasn't sure how I was going to make it another minute without turning one of them into a toad."

As if on cue, the musicians stuck up a tune just as they reached the dance floor. Dan held one of Aida's hands at eye-level between them and tucked his other arm behind his back, positioning himself for the traditional dance. As they started moving, he raised his eyebrows at her. "I thought you couldn't do anything to hurt another person."

"I can't hurt their *soul*," she corrected. "If a person is being a toad on the inside, sometimes it seems like it would be a service to make them look like one on the outside. In fact, affecting their physical body like that might do their soul some good in the long run."

A chuckle escaped him. "Remind me to never get on your bad side."

"Oh, don't worry. Of all the people in this and other worlds, you are the one person who has immunity."

The reminder of the lamp and his tie to it was a sobering punch in the gut. His lips pressed into a tight smile. "Right."

"But don't worry," Aida continued, apparently oblivious to his inner turmoil. "If I did turn one of them into a toad, I would make sure the magic could be undone. Maybe by a kiss of true love? Then they would have to actually learn what it means to earn someone's affection."

"Jasper was right: you're terrifying."

The words earned him a bright grin, and Dan was a lost cause for her.

There has to be a way to break the bindings that hold her. There has to be.

"Where is Jasper?" Aida looked over his shoulder, surveying the crowd of people. "I haven't seen him here tonight. I thought I expressly said in the invitation that you both were invited."

"He's at home. He said, and I quote, 'Unless there will be tigers, it sounds boring.'"

She snorted. "Glad to see he has his priorities in check. Do you think—"

She froze, and her eyes widened in shock and panic. "Dan? I—"

One second she was there, and the next she was gone, leaving behind nothing but a slight curl of lavender smoke.

Gasps of surprise echoed across the room. Dan looked at the place Aida had been standing just a moment before, then spun on his heel and took off running through the palace, his mind focused on just one thing:

The lamp.

A frantic Jasper met him at the door, crying and pacing in the front room. It took a moment to decipher his sobs, but Dan soon discovered the horrifying truth.

"There was a knock on the door after you left. I thought it might be Malik, because I told him I was free tonight and asked if he wanted to play a game or two of chatran. But it wasn't Malik; it was Hakim and Vizriel. Hakim had a torch and said he was going to burn the place down if I didn't give him the lamp. I told him that even if they did, it wouldn't matter because we could always get a new one. But then Vizriel laughed and said it would be hard for you to wish for anything from prison, and that Hakim had men at the palace waiting for a signal to arrest you, and that if I wanted to keep you from having a horrible 'accident' on the way to the magistrate's office, I needed to hand it over. I'm sorry, Dan. I'm so sorry. So, so, so sorry."

Dan did his best to comfort the boy, even as his own mind whirled with desperate, panicked thoughts.

"It's not your fault, Jas. We'll get her back."

"But what if we can't? What if I made her have to stay in the cave for another thousand years?" Jasper's breaths were quick and shallow, and his entire body shook. "What if she thinks that we don't love her?"

"We'll get her back," Dan said firmly. "And we'll make sure that she knows without a shadow of a doubt." He fidgeted with his ring, spinning it around on his finger as he offered up a desperate prayer that his words would not simply be false hope.

"Well now, what kind of trouble have the two of you gotten yourselves into this time?"

Dan let out a rush of pent up tension at the sound of Laelynn's voice. Jasper barreled into her, throwing his arms around her middle and burying his face. She gently stroked his hair as Dan quickly recounted everything that had happened.

"I'm going to get her back, but I don't know where they're going or how to catch up."

"Oh, that's simple enough." The fairy guardian looked around the shop for a moment before her eyes landed on one of the thick, woven rugs. "Well, why not?" she muttered to herself. "It worked with a pumpkin before, didn't it? A carpet shouldn't be too much different."

With a twist of her wrist and flick of her fingers, a sparkling rainbow of magic swirled through the air before settling into the carpet like a fine mist. The carpet immediately floated off the floor and hovered about two feet in the air.

"It's a magic carpet?" The reverent awe in Jasper's voice was counteracted by the hiccups that remained.

"It is," Laelynn replied with a cheerful smile. "All you need to do is direct it to take you to what your heart desires, and it will follow the quickest route there."

Dan wasted no time in gathering the carpet under his arms and heading for the door. Jasper detached himself from the fairy and followed at his heels. Just before exiting, Dan turned. "One more thing—the lamp. How do I break the binding that ties Aida to it?"

"There's a simple enough solution to that one, as well: you must wish for the one thing that seems impossible."

Fifteen

Aida

Aida paced across the small floor of her room, opening and closing her fists as frustrated, angry tears threatened to boil over. She had been tied to the lamp for long enough to know what the sudden summons meant.

She had a new master.

A disappointed, anguished groan escaped her, and she fell heavily to the pile of pillows on the floor.

"Why? Why now? I was so close. I was going to finally have the life I've always wished for. I was going to be a princess. Prince Kamaran was going to propose." She whispered the words into the empty space despite knowing that no one would ever hear them.

But is it really what I've wished for?

"It is." She stated the words firmly, arguing with herself. "Prince Kamaran might not be my first choice for a husband, but he definitely would never make me serve him."

What if he found out about the lamp? You know that no human can resist the allure of your magic.

"Except for Dan."

The thought crashed into her, carrying with it the weight of all her previous revelations about the confusing, wonderful man that she had so stubbornly pushed aside.

Like the way he so carefully chose his words to avoid making demands of her.

The way he never failed to offer her food or drink when she came to visit, even though he knew better than anyone that she was more than capable of taking care of herself.

The way he listened—truly listened—when she talked, as if what she had to say was the most important thing in the moment.

The way he often complimented her beauty, but never made her feel he was entitled to it.

The way he went out of his way to show her that he cared—escorting her back to the palace after her visits, making her a dress, using his wishes *for* her.

From the moment that they met in the cave, Dan had been a quiet, steadfast presence, offering her support and affection, even when she refused to believe she needed or deserved it.

And she loved him for it.

I love him.

The thought was at the same time terrifying and thrilling. Thrilling because she knew, beyond a shadow of a doubt, that Dan felt the same way about her. He had been showing it during every moment of their time together, not in words, but in action. Unlike everyone else that had come into her life over the last centuries, Aida knew that Dan's love wasn't built on the expectation of her magic. He had been given every opportunity to take it and run, and instead had remained for *her*.

It was terrifying because, now that she understood the truth of her own heart, she knew just how much it would destroy her to never see him again, to have the love that she had disregarded stolen out from under her fingers just when she realized how much of a treasure it actually was.

But I will see him again. Dan won't just let me be stolen away. He'll come for me; I know he will.

A warmth spread through her chest at the thought, filling her with strength and determination. It took a moment for her to recognize the foreign emotion.

It wasn't wishful thinking.

It was hope.

Her new master wore a different face but was just the same as all the rest. His eyes glowed with lust and greed, and the smile on his bearded face was predatory. He wore clothes that spoke of wealth, and the room that they stood in was furnished in dark wood and rich fabrics.

"Hello, Genie. I've been waiting for this moment for a long time. I thought it would be years again before I set eyes on your lamp, but imagine my surprise when I discovered that Dan and his little shadow didn't die in that cave as I had planned." He slowly and carefully tied the lamp to his belt.

This must be the man Dan wanted to avoid. Vizriel, I think his name was.

"But now you're finally mine!"

Aida fought the urge to roll her eyes, having heard some variation of the same speech too many times to count. She kept her expression bored and aloof.

Time for the script again, I suppose.

"Greetings, master. I am Aida, Genie of the lamp. Have you summoned me in order to receive your three wishes?"

Vizriel tilted his head, his eyes narrowing. "Is there another reason to summon you?"

"I have been told that I am a sparkling conversationalist."

He chuckled dangerously. "I have no need for conversation. I want three wishes."

Aida shrugged. "Very well. It's your loss." She nearly sighed in relief as the magic of the bargain wrapped around her, slightly loosening the hold of the lamp. "But you should be aware that my magic has limitations."

"Limitations?" He frowned.

She recited her spiel. "I can manipulate and change the natural world, but the spiritual is off-limits. I can't affect a person's soul. That also means that I can't alter other people's emotions or feelings, I can't kill anyone for you, and I can't bring them back from the dead. I also can't manipulate magic itself, so don't think you can go around asking for magical powers."

His face cleared. "Is that all?"

"Those are the boundaries of my magic. Choose your wishes wisely."

Or don't. The faster you blow through them, the less time I have to spend in your presence.

Vizriel rubbed his hands together gleefully. "I have already long considered what my wishes will be." He cleared his throat and stood tall, straightening his shoulders. "My first wish: I wish for a palace and wealth fit for a Sultan."

He went the riches route. Aida rolled her eyes. *So predictable.*

She closed her eyes, mentally picturing the fulfillment of his wish. A mischievous smirk pulled at the corners of her lips as the magic pulled words from her mouth. "Your wish is my command."

But the fool left the wish delightfully vague and open-ended.

Her eyelids opened and she snapped her fingers. Immediately they were surrounded by a palace of marble and gold, with polished floors and sparkling glass in the windows. Aida bit back a devious grin at the thought that Vizriel would soon find the floors in every other room so smooth and slick that staying upright would be impossible, and the glass in the windows so thin that the slightest pressure would break them. She furnished the inside as an almost exact replica of the Sultan's palace, but made one leg of every chair slightly shorter than the others so that they wobbled, and the tables two inches too low so that the bottoms would knock into the knees of whoever was seated. The soft feather mattresses on the beds were all slightly sloped towards the outside edges, and the silken cushions on every couch were lumpy. The silver spoons were too big to comfortably fit in one's mouth, and every knife in the place was dull.

Gasps of surprise from the other room filtered through the door, alerting Aida to the fact that Vizriel was not as alone as she thought. She quickly modified her plan, adding rubber grips to the bottoms of their shoes and making the servant's quarters the most comfortable in the palace.

*Abba knows they deserve it, having to deal with someone like **him** every day.*

Vizriel turned around slowly, his mouth spreading into a delighted smile as he took in his new surroundings. "Stupendous, utterly stupendous," he breathed. "Just as it should be."

Aida stood silently, hands clasped low in front of her. *Oh, yes. It **is** just as it should be.*

"Now for my second wish. I wish to be more powerful than even the Sultan!"

Wealth and power; why am I not surprised?

"Your wish is my command."

Aida snapped again, and a silver, bejeweled medallion appeared around his neck, denoting him as High Emperor—a title that, until that very moment, had never existed. A heavy crown materialized on his head...along with stacks of paperwork nearly three feet tall on the desk behind him. It wouldn't be long before the line of supplicants arrived.

Wait until he realizes that he will never have a day of peace again.

Vizriel stalked towards her, his eyes hungry. She instinctively took a step back.

"One wish left," he whispered. The back of her knees hit the edge of a low table, forcing her to stop. Vizriel's nose was inches from her face, and he gently ran the back of his fingers over her cheek.

She flinched away.

"Such exquisite beauty." He moved back a few inches and took his time looking her up and down. "And all mine."

Aida steeled herself. She reminded him, "You have one wish remaining."

Vizriel clasped his hands behind his back and began pacing the length of the room. Aida breathed in a deep sigh of relief as he finally retreated fully from her personal space. "It is an unfortunate limitation, three wishes. There is so much that must be left undone, unwished for."

She shrugged, never so glad in her life as she was in this moment that she had found the loophole of a bargain. "The rules are the rules."

"Ah, but see, with any rule there is always a loophole. You just have to think creatively enough to find it." He halted, turned on his heel, and fixed his dark, ambitious eyes on her. "The limit of three wishes is governed by your tie to the lamp."

A deep misgiving poured over her, but Aida said nothing.

"That means that, in order to supersede it, I must find a way to tie you to something else. Or some*one* else."

Her hands curled into shaking fists.

Dan, where are you?

Vizriel continued, a look of satisfaction stealing across his face. "There are some bonds that are stronger even than magic. For my third wish: I wish for you to be my bride."

Ice flooded through Aida's veins, and she felt as if she were suspended over a dark precipice with nothing to catch her.

"Wh-what?"

His eyes narrowed slightly. "I wish for you to be my bride."

Aida waited, but the compulsion to respond never came. Her heart slowly resumed beating at a normal pace.

"I said, I wish for you to be my bride!" Vizriel was growing angry, his face turning an impressive shade of purple. "You will be my bride! You will marry me, and then the magic governing your wishes will be tied to me instead."

"You must not have been listening carefully enough, Vizriel." Aida nearly melted in relief at the sound of Dan's voice as he strode into the room, Jasper following at his heels. His eyes searched the room until they found her, and the look in them was one of such warmth and reassurance that Aida had to restrain herself from running across the room and leaping into his arms.

He turned his attention back to Vizriel. "She clearly stated that she cannot fulfill a wish that harms another soul. I think forcing a girl into marriage to a man who clearly only sees her as a possession and a tool would certainly do that."

Sixteen

Dan

Dan breathed a prayer of thanks that he had been able to reach Aida in time. He glared at his former master, leaning into the rush of adrenaline that coursed through him after the wild, hair-raising race on the magic carpet to give him confidence. He still wasn't sure exactly how he and Jasper had arrived in one piece, but as it meant that he had been able to intercede right as things looked to be turning dangerous for Aida, he wasn't about to complain.

Vizriel's mouth curled into a sneer. "What are you doing here, street rat? Looking for something missing from your shop?"

Dan's eyes flicked to Jasper, and he made a subtle motion with his fingers towards the irate man. Jasper started slowly edging along the wall to position himself out of Vizriel's line of sight.

"I'm looking for some*one*," he answered, pointedly referencing Vizriel's earlier words. His eyes sought Aida again. "We never got to finish our dance."

"How sweet—the slave and the Genie," Vizriel sneered. "Am I supposed to be touched that you came all this way to reclaim her? She's mine now."

Jasper crept forward, keeping his movements small and noiseless. Vizriel, completely focused on Dan, did not register the boy's presence behind him.

I just need to keep him talking for a few more moments.

"But with only one wish left? Her usefulness to you will soon be over. How about a trade? You let Aida go free, and in exchange I will return to your service."

Even Dan knew that the idea was ridiculous, but he needed something to keep Vizriel's attention. Jasper was right behind him now, his pickpocket fingers slowly undoing the knot that secured the lamp to the man's belt.

"HA!" Vizriel barked. "This seems to be a habit of yours, boy—offering yourself in place of those you think to protect. Do you really think your measly skills are a fair exchange to the unlimited magic that I will soon be in possession of?"

The lamp slid off the rope and into Jasper's fingers, and he soundlessly leaped away, taking shelter against the wall near the door and hiding the lamp behind his back.

"But I must say, it's a habit that's rather convenient for me," Vizriel continued, completely unaware. "I recognized that ring on your finger for what it was the moment that I caught sight of it in the marketplace, but I also knew that such an heirloom was unlikely to be bought with the offer of gold alone. Thankfully Hakim was able to provide some insight into your relationship with that little urchin of yours, and I knew that all I had to do in order to secure you and the ring for myself was threaten to harm him. It worked like a charm. The moment you realized that Jasper would lose his hand, you threw yourself in front of him, practically offering yourself to me on a platter." He laughed cruelly. "I wish you could have seen your face."

"Your wish is my command."

Aida's words were spoken so softly that Dan was barely able to hear them. A second later, his hands were holding an oil painting depicting the scene in question: Jasper held by the guards, Hakim's blade swinging down, and Dan leaping between with an arm outstretched. The expression of mingled fear and desperation on his face was clear to see.

It took less than a second for Vizriel to realize what he had done. His eyes and mouth widened in horror. "No! NO!"

He reached for the lamp at his belt, only to find that it was gone. With a cry of rage, he jumped towards Dan, his hands outstretched and ready to strangle Dan's throat.

With a tiny puff of smoke, Vizriel disappeared, and a large cockroach scurried on the floor in his place. Its legs clicked on the marble floor as it ran in frantic circles before Dan's feet, then scuttled out the door.

Out in the hall, a woman's terrified shriek preceded the sound of crashing metal and a sickening crunch.

Dan and Jasper both looked at Aida with wide eyes. She shrugged. "I only turned him into a cockroach; I didn't hurt his soul." Her voice darkened. "To be honest, I'm not convinced he had much of one left."

The realization that Vizriel was gone, and that Aida was safe and sound finally sank in, and Dan crossed the space between them in three steps. He gathered Aida into his arms, holding her tightly and burying his face in her shoulder.

Thank you, Abba.

Jasper's arms wrapped around them both, and Dan took a moment to commit the feeling to memory.

Jasper was there.

Aida was safe.

It was everything he could wish for.

Almost.

Seventeen

Aida

If Aida had a choice, she would have spent the rest of her days encircled by the warmth and safety of Dan's arms. All too soon, his arms fell away, though he kept a hold of her hands. His deep brown eyes searched her face, love and concern plain to see. "Are you alright?"

She nodded, keeping her voice light in spite of the emotions that wanted to spill out. "I'm fine. It's nothing that hasn't already happened hundreds of times before. He was an odious, mean-spirited scoundrel who only sought gain for himself—just like all the rest."

Dan's lips pressed into a thin line, and his forehead wrinkled. "All of them?"

"Well, except for you, of course. You're neither odious nor mean-spirited. You're the least selfish human I have ever had the pleasure of knowing."

"I notice you didn't dismiss the idea of a scoundrel."

She gave him a teasing grin and leaned in closer. "Maybe I like the idea of a bit of roguishness. But don't worry, I know you're not really a scoundrel. You might have been a street rat when we met, but you're more of a prince than Kamaran is."

He blushed and dropped one of her hands to self-consciously rub the back of his neck. He cleared his throat. "How was it that you were able to change Vizriel like that? I thought as your master he was protected from you doing anything he didn't ask for."

"He made his final wish. When that happened, the bargain that we made was fulfilled, and he was no longer my master, and thus not under any sort of protection. I'm still tied to the lamp, but I am masterless now until the lamp is given to someone new."

Jasper and Dan exchanged a look, and Aida's stomach fell to her toes as all her previous elation was suddenly eclipsed by the horrifying realization that Dan still expected his third wish.

That's why he came after me. The voice in her head was as numb as her body. *It's not because he cares about me, but because he wants to make sure he gets his last wish.*

Her heart protested the thought, citing all the evidence and revelations she had explored while previously trapped in her lamp.

No. Dan wouldn't do that. He's not like that.

With unshed tears in her eyes and a hard lump in the back of her throat, Aida watched as Jasper solemnly presented the lamp to Dan. As soon as Dan's hands touched the metal, she felt the magic fall into place, tying them together once again. Dan refused to meet her eyes.

"We agreed upon three wishes, Aida, but I only got to use two."

No. Please, no.

His words felt like a stab to her heart, and the pain was so great that she could hardly breathe.

"And I know what I want for my third wish."

"What..." She swallowed thickly, willing the tears not to fall. "What is it?"

He finally looked up, and the light of love and adoration shining in his eyes was the last thing Aida had expected to see. He took her hands and wrapped them around the lamp, pressing it to her. "I want you to have a life of your own choosing, free from the constraints of magical bonds. I want you to fill it with joy and love and laughter and family. I want you to be free to satisfy the curiosity that burns in your eyes, to experience new things and see the world. I wish for your future, Aida." He took a deep breath before squeezing her hands one last time and adding, "And I hope that I can be a part of it."

As soon as Dan's wish was spoken, Aida felt the tension in the string-like magic that connected her to the lamp. It was like a tug-of-war, and the pressure in her chest squeezed and let up several times before, with one last pull, it broke completely.

Aida was free.

The lightness and relief were so beautiful and heady that she was tempted to just throw herself at Dan, wrap her arms around his neck, and kiss the man senseless, but the turmoil that he had put her heart through in the previous five minutes could not go ignored.

He was watching her closely, his face expectant and hopeful.

She kept her voice expressionless as she began the customary words. "Your wish..."

His face fell.

"...is mine, too."

It took a moment for her words to sink in, but with a whoop and a holler, Dan scooped her up and swung her about, sending the lamp clattering to the floor. Aida laughed, unable to contain her joy any longer.

He came to a stop, letting her slide slowly to the floor and keeping his arms around her waist. Her hands were on his chest, and she could practically feel the love that poured from him with every beat of his heart.

He touched her forehead with his own. "You're free."

"I'm free," she echoed. "And I'm yours."

And with those words, Aida found she didn't need to worry about kissing Dan senseless.

He was more than capable of returning the favor.

Epilogue

Aida

Aida stood still as a statue as Dan knelt on the carpet with a mouth full of pins and carefully marked the final hem of the white silk skirt that fell from her hips to the floor. The lace overlay would be cut to match once Dan was satisfied with the underneath layer, and Aida couldn't wait to see the finished product. The bodice was tailored perfectly to her body, with lace extended up all the way to her neck and down her arms in close-fitting sleeves.

Aida cleared her throat. "You know, I believe in some human cultures, it's considered bad luck for the groom to see the wedding dress before the ceremony."

"It is in Adhavi, as well." Dan spoke around the pins in his mouth, his fingers deftly moving as he folded the fabric and placed the last one.

Aida raised her brows. "Not worried about bad luck, then?"

"Not at all." Dan stuck the remaining pins into a pin-cushion beside his knees and pushed himself up from the floor. He circled Aida slowly, looking her over with the warm, adoring gaze that never failed to send a shiver of delight through her insides. "This isn't a wedding dress yet."

"It's not?"

"No. It's a beautiful dress on an even more beautiful woman, but until you wear it during the ceremony, it's not a wedding dress."

Aida laughed and gave his shoulder a light shove, and he responded by grabbing hold of her and pulling her into his arms. She leaned her head against him. "Those sound like Jasper-level reasoning skills."

"What can I say? I've learned from the best. His latest argument is that as long as you summon a mild-mannered tiger, it can hardly be called a wild animal, and therefore would be perfectly appropriate as a house pet."

"Maybe we should get him a cat."

"Maybe he should learn how to take care of his inanimate objects before we trust him with a living creature," Dan joked. "If he treats a pet the same way he does his sandals, forever leaving them in odd places and forgetting where, we will end up with a very cranky animal on our hands."

Aida laughed quietly along with him. She closed her eyes, reveling in the feel of him that never seemed to grow old. He was warmth and safety and love, and he was hers.

Thank you, Abba.

It had taken many, many hours spent in soul-searching and prayer, but Aida had finally come to the conclusion that, while her bondage to the lamp was truly and utterly abhorrent, she could still be thankful for the good that had come out of the situation.

After all, I got Dan and Jasper out of it.

"Are you ready for next week?" Dan's soft voice pulled her from her thoughts.

"More than ready. Though it is a little awkward having the wedding at the palace and knowing that Prince Kamaran will be there."

The Sultan, upon learning that Princess Aida had chosen to marry the tailor and would become a permanent resident of El-Huram, had immediately offered to host the wedding at the palace. He seemed to be just as eager to witness the ceremony as Aida and Dan were to participate in it. His fatherly presence helped soothe the ache in her heart at the absence of her own family from such an important moment. Now that she was free to travel any where she wanted, Aida could return home...but the thought of seeking out her family after all these centuries, after knowing that they had never once thought to question her disappearance—Aida wasn't sure she was ready for that reunion.

Not yet.

Maybe after they took Jasper up to the northern countries to look for *his* family.

"You're not disappointed that you're not marrying a prince?" Dan brushed his lips against her temple.

She forced the gloomy thoughts from her head and smiled up at him. "Not in the least. As it turns out, tailors are much more charming than princes."

"But they don't get to live in palaces."

Aida shook her head, rolling her eyes. "They could live in splendid townhomes if they wished."

Laelynn, after sending Dan and Jasper on their way on the magic carpet, had made it her business to ensure a copy of Vizriel's contract with Dan—signed at the bottom by Hakim as witness—had made it to the Sultan's desk. The chief magistrate had been swiftly stripped of all his power and sentenced to prison, and his home and properties offered to Dan as recompense.

Dan shrugged. "Too much space to keep clean, and the apartment upstairs is much closer to work."

"If only you knew someone who could keep it clean without a drop of effort."

He stepped back from her and looked her in the eyes, his expression serious. "I hope you know, Aida, that I will never make a decision with the expectation that you will use magic. Your powers are your own, and how you use them is up to you. If you lost your magic tomorrow, it wouldn't matter, because you are more than just a Genie. You are Aida, the woman I love with my entire being and the beautiful soul that, by this time next week, I will be blessed to call my wife. We can live wherever you want. I don't care, as long as I am with you."

"I love you, too."

The carpet underneath their feet shifted, and Aida lost her balance. She flailed her arms and started to fall backwards before Dan caught her, sweeping her into his hold with an arm around her back and one underneath her knees.

"What was that?"

"It seems Laelynn's magic carpet still has the ability to lead me towards my heart's desire." Dan tightened his hold on her and laughed. "Jasper did recommend that I try sweeping you off your feet." He waggled his eyebrows at her. "Do you think it worked?"

The smile that stretched across Aida's face was pure joy. Here, in Dan's arms, she knew that her desire for a happy ending was more than just a wish. It was a hope, an assurance, and her heart felt like it would burst with thankfulness.

There was only one thing that could make the moment better.

"Dan?"

"Yes?"

"I wish you would kiss me."

He set her down slowly, taking his time as he threaded his fingers through the hair on either side of her face, brushing her cheekbones with his thumbs. His words were a whisper against her lips.

"Your wish is my command."

Support the O.U.R.

The purpose of the "Hope Ever After" series is to spread hope and be an avenue to support and raise awareness in the fight against human trafficking and slavery. Here are some facts about human trafficking:

Every 30 seconds another person becomes a trafficking victim.

There are 40.3 million modern-day slaves estimated by the International Labour Organization. 1 in 4 slavery victims are children. 71% of slavery victims are women and girls.

Trafficking in persons is now the 2nd largest illicit industry in the U.S., 2nd only to the drug trade. It is also the fastest growing form of international crime. (UNICEF)

It is estimated that the human trafficking enterprise generates roughly $150 billion dollars a year.

The O.U.R. has aided in the arrest of over 4,000 predators, recovered over 6,000 survivors, and supported over 1,000 operations.

How can you help?

Educate yourself on how to recognize a victim of trafficking.

Take a stand against pornography, which leads the demand for sex trafficking.

Pray. Pray for victims and pray for those in the operations who are searching and rescuing victims

Buy all the books in the "Hope Ever After" series! All the proceeds from this series go to the O.U.R. to fight and end sex trafficking.

We hope our books inspire you to join the fight against human trafficking because God's children are not for sale. Thank you so much for your support!

> "The only thing necessary for the triumph
> of evil is for good people to do nothing."
> – Edmund Burke

> "Always remember, you have within you
> the strength, the patience, and the passion
> to reach for the stars to change the world."
> – Harriet Tubman

"There are three types of people: those who fight, those who help the fighter, and those who do nothing." – Dennis Prager

Acknowledgements

A huge thank-you first to Lei for spearheading and fear-lessly leading this project! Gathering and organizing and galvanizing a group of twenty authors is a massive un-dertaking, and you have done it all with such grace and kindness. This series has been a joy to be a part of, and I can't begin to express my gratitude and admiration.

Thanks as well to all the other ladies in the group, who have provided encouragement, laughter, and words of wisdom throughout this process. One of my favorite parts of collaborations is all the new friendships, and this journey has been no different!

A HUGE thank-you to my beta readers, Mary, Abby, and Bethany. This story was a bit of a diamond in the rough when you first saw it. Thank you for helping to make it shine!

And to my husband, Joe. This wouldn't be possible without you. I'm sorry Jasper didn't get his tiger...yet.

Above all, thanks and praise to Jesus Christ, our Living Hope. Soli Deo Gloria.

Also by Sarah Beran

Callie and the Pumpkin Seed (**Autumn Fairy Tales**)

To Crack a Soldier (**The Shattered Tales**)

A Wishful Hope (**Hope Ever After**)

Tales of Eukarya
Chords of Green and Gold
My Fair Mermaid
A Bond of Ice and Sunshine (coming 2024)

Seasons of Music and Magic
Spring of Sparkling Song: A Magic Flute Retelling
Summer of the Summoned Sword : A Lohengrin
Retelling
Fall of the Forgotten Phoenix: A Firebird Retelling
Winter of the Wandering Wind: A Flying Dutchman
Retelling

The Order of the Fountain
Second Star to the Right
Princess of the Beans
Maiden of the Sea
The Twelve Virtuosos
The Healer and the Huntsman
The Swan and the Slipper
Beauty from the Beast